NR

This book has not been rated. It contains harsh language and brief nudity. Read it at the risk of improving your mind.

Joseph William Szymanski (1906-2002)

"Napoleon III on a Fox Hunt, 1865-66," painted by Gustave Parquet (Born 1826 in Beauvais, France).

SPARROWS POINT

JOSEPH JOHN SZYMANSKI

iUniverse, Inc.
Bloomington

SPARROWS POINT

iUniverse books may be ordered through booksellers or by contacting:

iUniverse
1663 Liberty Drive
Bloomington, IN 47403
www.iuniverse.com
1-800-Authors (1-800-288-4677)

ISBN: 978-1-4697-6592-1 (sc)
ISBN: 978-1-4697-6593-8 (e)

Printed in the United States of America

iUniverse rev. date: 2/14/2012

Dedication

Because this novel may be my last as an author, it is dedicated to my father, Joseph William Szymanski, who gave 35 years to the Baltimore City Police Department without gaining a single stripe on the sleeve of his uniform. His life was a victory of courage under fire and against corruption within the department. It started with his first week on the job when a Captain ordered him to pick up *bag money* in a *dive* on the notorious *Block* of burlesque houses in downtown Baltimore. After refusing that order, the Captain and his aide, a Lieutenant, singled him out and gave him the worse assignments on the beat; anything to make his life as miserable as possible, hoping to break his spirit and get him to quit the force. From that time forward every day on the job was a fight for justice against injustice. His ethics were the highest and have always been an inspiration to me. The moral here is: "You don't need anything on your uniform to have courage and honor in your heart."

Acknowledgement

My gratitude is extended again to Michael McGrath of Windham, CT and Jeanie Woods of Mercersburg, PA for their critique and regenerative feedback. None of my books would have been published without their support and guidance, always accompanied with a declaration of praise and encouragement.

To paraphrase Charles Dickens' David Copperfield, whether or not I shall turn out to be a good writer depends on factors beyond my control. If I am judged by the number of books sold, it's a foregone conclusion that I should have devoted six years to running my art business instead of writing BETTERTON, ROCK HALL, ABERDEEN, and SPARROWS POINT. If, however, after I am dead, a producer or director elects to make any of my books into a movie or television series, then I will have the last laugh and be turning in my grave. Only time will tell. The clock is always ticking, even when you're dead.

Preface

My three previous novels, *BETTERTON, ROCK HALL* and *ABERDEEN*, were created from recollections of characters I've known during a 42-year career as an appraiser and art dealer. However, *SPARROWS POINT* was based on an idea about a specific place in Baltimore, my home town. Most of the events in the storyline are true and autobiographical, but fictionalized to protect the real names of places and individuals living or dead.

After graduating in February 1952 from Patterson High in Highlandtown, Southeast Baltimore, my sandlot baseball coach Sheriff Fowble, a supervisor at Bethlehem Steel at Sparrows Point, used his influence to get me hired as a draftsman. It was a *cushy* job that required sitting at a drafting table and studying blueprints until my eyes became blurred. Those first eight hours, perched in a second floor loft, seemed like a lifetime and after clocking out, I never went back for my pay. The terrible stench and putrid odors rising from furnaces, moist concrete pads and leaky, rusty pipes were too much to bear.

That experience was forged into my psyche and made me work harder in whatever I would do for the rest of my life. Any job would be better than rotting away in that loft although Sheriff Fowble never complained about his job or the vapors inside the mill. He was a great baseball coach and pro scout for several major league teams, but to this day, I wonder how he could endure working at *Sparrows Point* for over 30 years. By the way, everyone pronounced it *Sparris Point.*

During my lifetime, clichés from Sheriff often popped up when the occasion warranted their usage. One of his favorites was shouted at the top of his lungs (long before Leo Durocher said it) when a pitcher on the opposing team ran out of steam on his fastball: "Stick a fork in him; he's done."

After a year of hard labor and realization that SPRROWS POINT was ready for submission to iUniverse, I sometimes imagine that he was referring to me.

Chapter 1

Our story begins on an unusually warm April 1st as a gaggle of Canada geese fly along Eastern Neck Island Road (ENIR), heading south out of Rock Hall, a small town on the Eastern shore of Maryland. Along the way they swerve in a zigzag pattern and honk to one another as their eyes measure the growth of the soybean and corn fields below. On the right of ENIR is a string of 30-to-50-acre farms fronting the Chesapeake Bay; on the left are larger ones, such as the approximate 4,000 acre *DuPont* farm, facing the Chester River.

Eventually, the geese pass over a large wooden sign on the right side of ENIR. Its florescent lettering reads: 'Welcome to Maryland's EASTERN NECK ISLAND WILDLIFE REFUGE.' A northwesterly breeze blows up the Bay from the Atlantic Ocean and makes the sign sway slightly, producing an eerie screech from the rusty links in its chain. As the wind fades away, a red-breasted robin, a rose-breasted grosbeak, a chickadee and a finch, a quartet with the best voices in the Refuge, called the *Chordettes,* fly out of the woods and settle on top of the sign. It's Showtime; a noontime routine in which all the birds in the Refuge stop whatever they're doing and wait to hear their unique harmonizing.

After spotting a pigeon with a stripped underbelly named Mandel "Mandy" Sandman flying overhead, the *Chordettes* know it's their cue to begin chirping an old melody:

"Mr. Sandman, bring us a dream, make him the cutest that we've ever seen, give him two lips like roses and clover, then tell him that his lonesome nights are over. We're so alone, don't have nobody to call our own, please turn on your magic beam, Mr. Sandman, bring us a dream.

"Make him the cutest that we've ever seen, give him a pair of eyes with a 'come-hither' gleam and the word that we're no rover, then tell him that his lonesome nights are over.

"We're so alone; don't have nobody to call our own. Mr. Sandman, please turn on your magic beam. Mr. Sandman, bring us a dream."

After the *Chordettes* finish their song, Mandy is joined by three other pigeons, all flying at a height of about 50 feet in a tight diamond formation, with hardly any space between their wing tips. From the ground they resemble a squadron of Navy jets known as the *Blue Angels*. Suddenly Mandy rolls his wings to indicate that he heard their harmonizing and will try to bring them a dream later, on his way back to the Refuge.

After passing out of the forest and over its small beach, the squadron climbs to an altitude of 200 feet and levels off at a speed of 45 mph. The pigeons break formation and peel off in four directions, with Mandy, the lead one, going forward and the one in the rear making a 180-degree turn and heading back to the Refuge, probably for a lustful afternoon of splendor in the grass.

Fifteen minutes later, Mandy glances at his wing tip vortices to make sure they're in the up position to conserve energy in this afternoon's long flight plan. "Avian specialists claim that male pigeons with their wing-tip vortices pointed upward are the result of erotic thoughts, emanating from the God Eros," he says to himself. "That claim is all nonsense because I have erotic thoughts all the time, even when I'm not in flight!"

The screen of his GPS guidance system flashes across his eyes and gives off a short burst of beeps to confirm that he's almost halfway across the Chesapeake Bay and approaching a change in course. Suddenly, an enormous burst of thunder causes him to stop flapping and lower his ailerons, a smart decision since lightning strikes the area directly in front of him. When he looks down, a spirit rises out of the bay; it's a short, trim man who resembles a white-bearded rabbi, wearing a long robe that hides his feet and sparkles from the dazzling flashes of light reflected off its iridescent-gold threads.

"*Ya* know how much this robe costs a yard?" he asks Mandy in a heavy Yiddish accent. "Over three dollars a yard and I can't afford to wear it anymore when I'm in the *Chesepiook*, the name given by the Algonquin Indians to the Chesapeake. Try pronouncing that in Yiddish and I'll make you one of my converts. Anyhow, one minute I'm in salt and the next in fresh water. But *ya* certainly picked a good day to go flying, *goy*."

"Are you the Spirit of the Chesapeake *Bay*?" asks Mandy.

"*Ya hoyd* of me?"

"Everyone in flight school has *hoyd* about you. That's all they talked about during breaks between classes, mainly when we're on the crapper," he says, giggling. "What are you doing out on the bay at noon? I know you're always looking for converts. Don't tell me you're also directing traffic?"

"What *chutzpah*," says the Spirit in a quick retort.

"As a putz," says Mandy, "I was only trying to gain some confidence and courage."

"And what's wrong with directing traffic?" the Spirit asks in a rising crescendo. "You should also know that I was a traffic cop at the crucifixion in charge of crowd control, but that's another story. No one should ever forget their roots. Where *ya* headed?"

"I'm on my way to *Balamer* because it's a perfect 75 degrees, unusual for the first of April. But I don't need your help since I'm equipped with GPS."

"*Oy* gevalt! That's what you think, you little *schlemiel,"* says the Spirit. "That's what they all say before colliding in space. Trust me. You will always need clearance from a flight controller when you fly over any part of the largest estuary in America. Have you forgotten its 64,000 square miles? *Un zo*, I'm giving you permission to maintain your current air speed and altitude, but make a 90-degree right turn here and head north until you reach the mouth of the

Patapsco River. You can relax after making a gradual 45-degree left turn because tail winds will help you glide all the way to the Inner Harbor. After reaching the port of Baltimore, you're on your own, *klutz*. By the way, if you happen to run across a former Navy SEAL named Mark Hopkins whose Ridgefield Farm is next to your fight school, give him my best regards. *Mazel Tov* to you and him and whoever's still reading this book."

"Thanks a load," says Mandy as another flash of lightning strikes near the Spirit who spins like a top and disappears into the Bay, leaving only a descending swirl of white mist. "Meeting the Spirit over the middle of the Bay is fantastic and almost enough to knock the crap *outta* a bird like me, but the Bay below is already polluted enough from the runoff of pesticides on lawns of waterfront homes to keep me in flight."

Thirty minutes later Mandy passes Sparrows Point on his right and Fort McHenry and the giant 'DOMINO Sugar' sign on his left. After descending to about 50 feet, he approaches the helipad at the Inner Harbor and circles it to get his next bearing, which is to glide across Pratt Street and head north along Eutaw Street. Five blocks later, after reaching the intersection of Lexington and Eutaw Streets, he veers to the right and lands next to a female dove with a large white-gray cere (nostrils) on her beak.

Both are perched on the top of the last letter of a 10-foot high by 30-foot-wide sign, protruding from the Eutaw-Street entrance of a red-brick, two-story, square block building; it's shiny brass letters spell out the building's name, 'LEXINGTON MARKET.' Mandy turns his head, leans over to the dove and says, "Would you hold it against me if I said your body suits me to a T?"

"Cut it out, *hon*," says the dove. "It's the first Saturday in April and although spring is in the air, I don't have time for *cooing* and all that mush and foreplay. I didn't sleep at all last night and I'm as hungry as a prairie fox. Right now I'd settle for a peanut from Konstant's Nut House or any crumbs from the other vendors inside the market."

"You don't want any *yakety-yak* or *cooing*?" asks Mandy. "That's regrettable."

"Regrettable? That's downright preposterous for someone of my standing," she says, giving him a nudge to back away slightly so she has a better view of who's going in or out of the market. "By the way, I haven't seen you around these parts. You must be a new guy in town and from your accent, I'd say you hail from south *Balamer*."

"Affirmative, honey bun. I just got my wings after graduating *summa cum laude* from fight school at the Eastern Neck Wildlife Refuge outside Rock Hall."

"I heard about that place. They must feed you air-cadets high protein supplements. You're a little hefty between the armpits."

"If you were outfitted with the latest telemetry, such as Global Positioning System (GPS) and a Norden bombsight, you'd look a little beefy too. And I was born with a big heart."

"Ah, that makes you one of the new breed of flyers, the space-age ones they call 'Top Gun.' What brings you to downtown *Balamer*?"

"I *hoyd* about Lexington Market," says Mandy, "and wanted to get a good look before heading back to *Sparris Point* to team-up with a squadron of seagulls to complement the *ebouys* positioned offshore. We're part of a task force to monitor pollutants in the Bay, but aircraft-carrier pigeons like me are always on call for emergencies when there's a power outage."

She pauses to use her beak to scratch her chest and says, "By the crowd of people rushing into the market, you wouldn't know that we're in a recession."

"Are you sure you wouldn't enjoy a pause for some necking?"

"Necking is permissible but you know how easily it can get *outta* hand," she tells him. "You certainly come on strong after meeting someone for the first time. As I told you before, I'm hungry for food, not love."

"I come on strong because I don't believe in *beating around the bush*. Time is too precious to waste. But I never expected to hear a dove tell me she preferred food over sex."

"You're trying awfully hard to get me in the *nest*. As I said before, *bug wit*, it *is* Saturday, the busiest day of the week."

"In that case, perhaps you'll pardon me while I relieve myself."

"You better think twice about dropping your *do-do* here," she tells him.

"Even if it's on that guy wearing the New York *Yankees* baseball cap and jacket with the name, Heathcliff, woven on the back of his collar?"

"While you're *wuthering* from great *heights*, don't take aim on him or the guy next to him, wearing a Boston *Red Sox* cap and jacket with the name 'Paulo Revere' woven on the back of his collar. They're probably rich tourists taking in a baseball game at *Oryuls Park* tonight. This area is classified as a safe zone, under the protection of Homeland Security. If you *do-do* here, it's bad manners and would give *Charm City* a bum rap for letting pigeons hang out around the market."

"Good advice, hon. You go on ahead. Do whatever you *do-do* on a Saturday at noon."

"No one tells me what or when to *do-do* or not to *do-do*. I'm '*numero uno*' around this market. I'll *do-do* on you if you don't cut the pigeon talk!"

Chapter 2

As Paulo gets to a spot about ten feet away from the entrance door, directly below the sign of the market, he tells Heathcliff, "That six-block hike uphill from the Hyatt at the Inner Harbor worked up my appetite."

"The bell boy said that there's no better place to eat than Lexington Market," says Heathcliff as he pushes open the heavy glass doors to the east side of the market.

Both quickly survey the first stall that occupies about 2,000 square feet. "Get a good whiff of whatever's being fried," says Paulo. "The food must be good if it's still here after 225 years. I mean the market's been here that long, not the food."

"This place is packed," says Heathcliff, "even tighter than Yankee Stadium."

"Ah, so this is Faidley," says Paulo, leading Heathcliff to customers in line for fried seafood. "They're supposed to be famous for their backfin and jumbo-lump crab cakes. Something tells me that it's going to be difficult to decide what to eat first, but this looks like a good start."

Paulo places two orders for jumbo lump crab cakes and two beers and laughs when the lady hollers 'two jumbos' to a cook, who quickly retrieves two crab cakes from a refrigerator and carefully places them into the strainer of a deep fryer.

A few minutes later Heathcliff and Paulo are standing side by side in the middle of a row of wood countertops, slowly savoring their order of crab cakes with a side order of Coleslaw and a pickle.

"Did you notice in the middle of Faidley's stall the oyster bar lined with customers leaning over and slurping down raw oysters on the half shell?" asks Heathcliff. "Look at the two shuckers behind the counter. I clocked one of them who took only five seconds to open three and pass them on a plate to a customer. Talk about high speed work. Those guys are jet-propelled."

"How about an order of oysters as a second appetizer?" asks Heathcliff.

"I'll pass, thank you. No oysters for me, even if they're served with lemon juice or Tabasco."

"You're passing up an extraordinary experience. They're considered an aphrodisiac and will increase your sex hormones and testosterone," says Heathcliff, nudging him with his elbow.

"What in the hell are you talking about?" asks Paulo. "Our girls are out shopping and spending our money and you're thinking about sexual enhancement so early in the day?"

"As Freud said, 'a man has continuous mental manifestations or flashes of an erotic nature,'' Heathcliff answers quickly and smiling. "Thinking about sex reminds me of a story about two woodpeckers."

"I don't believe I've heard that one," says Paulo. "Run that by me, please."

"The story begins in the forest of the Eastern Neck Wildlife Refuge on the Chesapeake Bay," says Heathcliff. "A woodpecker is having trouble pecking a hole in a tree and says out loud, 'I guess my pecker is not what it used to be. Wish I had one of those performance enhancing drugs for men who can't get their pecker hard when they need to.' He looks up to a higher limb and sees a younger woodpecker carefully watching him. 'Can I be of any help, old-timer?' he asks."

Suddenly Paulo decides to tease his friend and asks, "By the way do you have any trouble getting your pecker hard when you're away from home?"

"If I stop to give you an answer, it will spoil the punch line of this story," says Heathcliff. "So permit me to continue, please."

"The older woodpecker says, 'I don't recognize you, stranger. You're not from around these woods, are you?'

"The younger one answers, 'Affirmative, but that shouldn't prevent me from being a Good Samaritan. I was told this is a friendly forest.'

"The older one says, 'It is. To deny your help would be considered bad behavior on my part. Of course, I'd be happy if you lend me your beak.'

"Finally, the foreign woodpecker flies down to the spot where the older woodpecker tried to peak a hole and begins pecking. Within a few seconds, he bores a big hole into the tree and says, 'It's amazing how hard your pecker gets when you're away from home!'"

"I'm sorry I asked to hear it," says Paulo, shaking his head and swallowing the last half of his Anchor Steam beer. "If I were a scorekeeper, Faidley would score a hit with their crab cake. But this is only the first inning. *Whataya* want to try next?"

After a pause, they shrug their shoulders and throw up their hands, surrendering to their gastronomical dilemma. Finally Heathcliff says, "You talked me *outta* having oysters, but the crab cake from Faidley's *was* a winner. We're on a roll, 'crab-wise' as Billy Wilder would say. How would a juicy pastrami sandwich on rye suit you?"

"The bell boy said we should try Mary Mervis Deli," Paulo answers. "We could see how their pastrami compares to Cantor's in Greenwich Village, sandwich-wise."

They walk down an aisle, passing Polock Johnny's stall on the right side and pausing to inhale the aroma of fat oozing out of sausages on the grill. Seconds later they face a crowd of people coming up the aisle with no way to pass them, and are forced to the right, facing *Berger's Bakery* with their showcases displaying a wide of cakes and pies. They inhale a whiff of the freshly-fried cinnamon glazed doughnuts and can't resist buying a dozen.

Eventually Heathcliff and Paulo maneuver into the third row of customers around Mary Mervis Deli. A sign in the center of the-stall reads: 'We've been satisfying customers since 1913'. On display in five-foot-high refrigerated showcases, completely encircling the stall, are a wide variety of high quality meats, cheeses and salads, each labeled with a price per pound. Behind the showcases are at least five workers, moving like a well-orchestrated team. In the corners are meat slicers, running continuously and slicing wafer-thin portions of pastrami, corned beef and kosher ham that workers grab by a handful, often without weighing on a scale and slap it on a roll faster than you can say 'Jackie Robinson.'

A short, stocky, middle-aged waitress with her hair tied in a bun and muscles bulging under her short-sleeves, counts out the change and hands it along with a paper bag to a waiting customer. "OK, who's next?" she shouts, wiping her gloved hands on her soiled apron.

"I am," answers Mark Hopkins, a handsome, six-foot four-inch, 30-year old who resembles Cary Grant in his prime; he wears the gold-plated trident emblem of the Navy SEALS on his collar, leans closer to the glass showcases and hollers, "Shrimp salad on a hoagie roll."

In less than 10 seconds she uses her right hand to jam an ice-cream-trigger scooper into a stainless-steel pan of shrimp salad with home-made dressing oozing out. She spreads two scoops on a fresh roll held in the palm of her left hand, wraps the hoagie in a special cellophane paper and slides it into a takeout bag. The entire process is synchronized robotic perfection, completed in less than 30 seconds. No time or energy was wasted and not a word spoken or sung by the waitress.

"Anything else, *hon*?" she asks, smiling and suddenly feeling the urge to flirt. "How about a corned beef on rye or I? In case you didn't catch my drift, it rhymes."

"I catch your drift, but I'm a happily-married man. As for the corned beef, maybe next time," he answers then feels a bump from someone pushing him from behind.

"Give it back. Give it back or I'll break your arm!" says a slender man standing behind Mark; he appears to be about 40 and is dressed in a pink polo shirt and dungarees.

Mark turns around to see that the man has a teenager by the throat.

"What's all this commotion about?" Mark asks, using his fists to break the man's stranglehold. "You should try picking on someone your own size, not a kid."

"Give the man back his wallet, the one you took from his back pocket," says the man.

The five-foot eight-inch, 15-year old teenager begins to shiver, reaches inside his unbuttoned shirt and hands Mark his wallet. "Is this what you're looking for, the one you dropped on the ground?"

"You don't get off that easy," says the man. "Apologize to him for taking it and lying, otherwise I'll turn you over to security."

The kid steps back from the huddle around Mary Mervis' stall and says, "I'm sorry and especially sorry for getting caught."

"Beat it, kid," says the man, watching the teenager disappear in the crowd, "and stay away from here. Pickpockets like you give the market a bad name."

"Here's a twenty, buy yourself a sandwich and drink and meet me upstairs in the mezzanine," says Mark. "I'll get us a table and wait to hear more about what happened here."

A few minutes later at the mezzanine balcony overlooking the ground floor of the market, the man in the pink shirt takes a seat. Mark takes a big bite into his shrimp-salad sandwich. When he finishes licking his lips as some dressing spills out of the corners of his mouth, he says, "I'm Mark Hopkins. What's your name?"

"Glen Glenn," he answers quickly. "It's nice to meet you."

"What was all that commotion with the teenager? Was he a pickpocket?"

"Yes, I would say he was, but not a very good one."

"I don't see you with a sandwich or drink."

"I'd rather save the money you gave me for later."

"Here is half of mine," he says. "They're big enough for two people anyway. Don't tell me you're out of a job?"

"You got that right."

"Tell me something about yourself."

"I'm thirty and spent ten years with the *Balamer* City Police Department (BCPD) until two months ago when I was laid off along with 200 other men and women due to budget cutbacks."

"You don't seem to fit the image of a policeman on one of the best forces in America. You're barely five foot nine-inches and 150 pounds."

"Size is not important, at least not with me. How do *you* take the measure of a man?"

"My father told me that a man is measured by the number of friends he has."

"I didn't ask you about how your father measured a man. I asked you how you go about it."

"I believe a man has to prove himself to be a man, every day, every time he faces a challenge. And I didn't mean to imply that I take the measure of a man by his size, age or color of his skin. You get my meaning?"

"Affirmative."

"Now tell me more about your work with the BCPD."

"I started by walking a beat, and then rode a motorcycle and drove a patrol car, mostly to accidents until the blood from fatalities gave me headaches and nightmares. Eventually they transferred me inside to a desk job, helping detectives track down suspects in criminal cases."

"I might have a job for you, provided everything you've told me is the truth. We're developing a small marina on the eastern shore of the Chesapeake Bay and looking for someone special for security and maintenance. But you'll have to take an interview with our manager, Womble Weinstein. He has approval of all new-hires, but a recommendation from me may be helpful."

After shaking his hand and wishing him good luck, Mark jots down Womble's name and telephone number at Ridgefield on his business card and hands it to him. As he walks over to the nearest trash bin, he passes a table where Heathcliff and Paulo are finishing their sandwich. Mark stops momentarily to tell Heathcliff, "I hope your Yankees will take it easy tonight on the Orioles, maybe let them win a game."

"If you're an Orioles fan," says Heathcliff, "you're in the minority. They're a tricky team and you never can tell what they're going to do. If they find a way to hit in the clutch with runners on base and keep bringing up young pitchers from their farm system, they may be a team to fear in a few years."

"That's too much of a goal," says Mark. "Enjoy the game and may the best team lose for once in a blue moon."

A few minutes later, Mark is standing in front of a bin of hard-shell crabs at Faidley's stall. Because of all the noise, he has to cup his hands around his mouth to shout out his order to a helper behind the bin, "What will a dozen Number 1 Bluefin's cost me today?" he asks, leaning over the bin to hear the answer.

"Forty dollars a dozen," says the attendant. "We just got in ten bushels from a waterman since it's unusually warm for this time of the year."

"I know that it's the beginning of the season for watermen but I don't want to pay a premium. I'll take a dozen, make sure they're alive before you steam them and don't forget the heavy seasoning with pepper."

While waiting for his order, he catches a glimpse of Glen who is standing near the entrance to the market and handing money to the same teenager who tried to steal his wallet. When he sees Mark approaching, the teenager dodges around clusters of people leaving the market until he's completely out of sight.

"What's going on here, Glen?" Mark asks suspiciously.

"That's personal and I prefer to keep it that way."

"Well, as far as I'm concerned, it's not personal because it includes me, and you better explain yourself fast, otherwise I may jump to the wrong conclusion and turn you over to security for questioning."

"The teenager is my son. You may think it's a scam but it isn't, believe me. It's an operation that relies on our getting a tip for returning the wallet. We wouldn't steal anyone's wallet."

"That's a *helluva* way to make a buck, especially when it involves your son. You should be ashamed of yourself. What kind of message and example are you giving him? How can he respect you or himself? What's your son like?"

"He likes girls with big tits!" says Glen, laughing and trying to add some levity to a serious conversation.

"Most teenage boys are like him. Who does he take after?"

"Girls with big tits," Glen says again. "But you must know that when you're *down and out*, someone will resort to anything short of murder. Frankly, I wouldn't blame you if you turned me over to security. You were the first person we tried *it* on and it will be the last, I promise you."

"This is not the time and place for us to talk things over, but if you still want a job and can pass the interview, nothing has changed. You've come clean and I've always believed that a person should get a second chance. But one thing I will not tolerate is a lie. In combat, in the military, a lie can take the life of a soldier. If I can't trust you, I want nothing to do with you. Do you understand?"

"Yes, I do. I could have told you that it was all an April Fools' Day joke, but it wasn't. You can be sure that I won't pull that dumb stunt again."

"Now that I think more about it, write up everything that you did and said today as if you're writing a segment for a Broadway play or Hollywood script; but change your character into drag. In other words, instead of you being a man, you're a woman with a big purse that you threaten to use on the teenage-pickpocket. When you get it all down on paper, call Womble at Ridgefield and give it to him as part of your interview for a security job at Swan Haven Marina in Rock Hall. We might use it in a film project under development at Ridgefield Studio, a subsidiary of Ridgefield Farm. Womble will explain it all to you when you take your interview."

"I don't know what to say except 'Thank You'. You can tell Womble to expect my call at nine on Monday morning," says Glen, relieved and grateful that Mark has offered him a second chance.

"And here's a little something to carry you over the weekend and expenses when you drive to Ridgefield Farm for your interview," says Mark, pushing a $100-dollar bill into the upper pocket of Glen's shirt. "I feel as if I rescued someone who's going to be a good friend if he wises up. Don't disappoint me, Glen."

When Mark returns to pick up his crabs, the attendant tells him, "I picked out the heaviest ones myself. No *windbags* in this dozen, Sir."

"*Way-da-go*," says Mark, handing him two twenty-dollar bills with his right hand and a five-dollar tip with his left.

Chapter 3

A few minutes later, Mark is walking through the market's parking lot and holds the hot crabs up to his nose to smell the aroma still coming through the double-lined paper bag. He remembers how those blue-fin hard-shell crabs are caught, seasoned and eaten because he learned it from his father who took him on trips to the Chesapeake Bay after he was able to swim on his own. He licks his lips because he still recollects the taste of their special sweet meat that was fed to him as a child in a high chair.

After placing the hot bag carefully in the trunk of his BMW, he covers it with a blanket and, before he pushes the ignition switch, says to himself, "I haven't been to Howard Street in a long time. I wonder what Thaynes might have inside his dusty antique shop. Think I'll swing by on my way back to Cylburn."

After Mark finds a parking spot in the middle of 'Antiques Row,' a name given to the one-block of three-story houses converted into shops, he walks into the one on the corner.

"I thought this was Thaynes Antiques," he says to a young lady behind a waist-level glass counter with costume jewelry on display in the center of the store.

"It used to be but not anymore," she tells him. "I've only been working here a year but heard he faded away."

"I can't begin to imagine how Thaynes could 'fade away,' as you say, since he weighed at least 250 pounds and stood about five foot eight," Mark tells her. "He stood out like a buoy bobbing in the Bay. I had a big score a few years ago when he sold me a painting by the Finnish impressionist painter, Albert Edelfelt."

"Look around. You might find another big bargain to brag about. Everything in the shop is donated to Women in Need (WIN) to raise funds for battered women. Here's our card in case you'd like to donate something."

Mark takes his time to meander slowly through the shop and remembers kicking a painting that Thaynes had leaning against a cabinet in the back of his shop. In a quick flashback, he visualizes the excitement when his eyes first saw the artist's brushstrokes in the painting of a beautiful young lady reading a book under a shady tree. "Images of something original and better executed than Monet are something you never forget," he says to himself. "Maybe I'll get lucky again."

After getting a good look at almost everything in the shop, he ends up in the front section again and faces the lady, who is now resting on a three-foot high, arts and craft stool. "Did you find anything that interests you, Sir?" she asks.

"I'm curious about the baby doll in that cabinet over there," Mark says, pointing to his right. "I noticed that you keep it locked."

After they walk over and the lady uses a pass key to open the glass doors, she hands him the doll. Mark turns up the hair covering the back of the doll's neck to read what's written there by the manufacturer. "Can you tell me anything about it?"

"Actually, it was my mother's doll and she never let me play with it. For as long as I can remember it was always inside a cabinet, like this one, in our living room. As far as I know, it's in original condition. I even have the box it came in when my grandmother purchased it in 1912 from Hochschild Kohn."

"And what is the price?" asks Mark.

"Three hundred fifty dollars," she answers quickly then pauses to add, "and remember, the money goes to a good cause."

"I'll take it. You twisted my arm. It'll be a birthday present for our little girl, Baby Ruth."

"I'm pleased that it will have a good home," she says.

As Mark reaches into his jacket and begins to take out his checkbook, he notices a dachshund walking slowly from behind the counter and follows it over to the front of the shop where it stops and begins to lift its rear leg to urinate on a bronze placed there as a door stop to keep the front door open.

"Hey, young fella, that's not meant to be urinated on! Where are your manners and appreciation of art?" he says, carrying it outside to use a tree in front of the store. The dachshund lifts his leg and urinates on a newspaper lying beside the tree; the headline reads: "Yankees Sweep Birds Again!"

"That little rascal; I should give Rudy a good scolding," says the lady behind the counter after the dog meanders cowardly behind the front jewelry showcase. "I forgot to let him relieve himself outside before opening the shop at 11:00. We're renting the apartment over the shop."

"When you *gotta* go, you *gotta* go," Mark tells her, having a closer look at the bronze.

"We just got it in this morning. Someone came by and just consigned it with a note telling us: 'Check it out and don't take less than $800 for it.'"

"There's something familiar about this bronze," he says.

"You don't have to play cat-and-mouse with me. You know what it is: *The Broncho Buster* by Fredric Remington. It's probably a recast made in China where everything is being copied today. Did you know that they bury the bronzes in a pit of urine to age them?" she tells him, giggling and covering her mouth sheepishly.

"You talked me into buying it," says Mark, handing her a check for $1,150 for the doll and bronze.

Because he is relishing in his discovery of the Remington bronze as if he just found a winning lottery ticket, Mark is not the least perturbed by the traffic on Howard Street and Charles Street, which changes the drive time from 15 to 30 minutes. After setting the bag of crabs on the kitchen counter at Cylburn, he gives his mother, Sara, and his wife, Lola, a hug and kiss.

"For dinner?" asks Lola, opening the bag to have a peek and releasing the aroma of the seasoned crabs.

"The Broncho Buster" by Frederic Remington (American 1861-1909).

"Hold onto your appetite a little longer," says Mark, giving her a long kiss. "I have something for you and Baby Ruth out in the car. I'll be back in a jiffy."

When he returns, Mark is carrying a baby doll in one hand and the Remington bronze in the other. "This is a present for my two babies," he says, handing the baby doll to Lola.

"She's a living doll," says Lola, holding it up for Sara to see too. "She's almost as beautiful as Baby Ruth."

He places the Remington bronze on the large sill of a pop-out window in the kitchen where sun streaming through the bay window casts its light on the action of a cowboy trying to break a wild horse. "Here's an important bronze to augment our collection of American art," says Mark. "Remington gave the cowboy a special place in the history of *cow-poking.* It takes more than courage to grip the mane of a roaring stallion as it rears up on its hind legs while his right arm is outstretched for balance."

"It symbolizes all that was heroic and triumphant in the old West," says Lola, touching the hind quarters of the broncho. "As the horse tries to toss him, only his left foot is still in the stirrup, and he's holding a horse quirt (braided rawhide) in his right hand."

"You could give me a million dollars," says Sara, "and I wouldn't trade places with him. What a way to earn a living. Broncho-busters must have busted more than just a wild stallion. I bet they busted their, ah, dare I say it?"

"Say it, Mom, or better yet, I'll say it," says Mark, laughing; "Ass."

"I doubt if you were thinking of Haussner's when you bought it," says Sara, gloating a bit, "but seeing it in the window sill reminds me of the bronzes that Haussner's Restaurant had on display in their windows along Clinton Street. I still cannot believe they sold all their art for over twelve million dollars after they closed their doors yet never owned anything by Remington, Russell or Fraser."

"Everyone has their own tastes in life and in collecting art," says Lola. "Luckily for us, Mark has a wider perspective and appreciation of America and its painters and sculptors."

While his wife and mother are conversing, he asks to be excused to go to his study and over the Internet find out what Wikipedia has to say about the bronzes of Remington.

According to *www.fredericremington.org*, Mark learns that Remington achieved instant acclaim when a 23 1/2-inch-high bronze was produced by the sand-cast process in 1895 by the Henry-Bonnard Bronze Company of New York. It was Remington's first attempt at sculpting and some bronzes were sold at Tiffany's. After the Rough Riders bought a copy and presented it to President Theodore Roosevelt, Remington was ecstatic and his fame began to spread throughout America. Around 1900 Roman Bronze Works (RBW) of New York was authorized to cast bronzes with the lost-wax process and continued producing them after the death of his wife in 1918.

"Only the log books and ledgers of Henry-Bonnard and RBW can tell the full story of each casting from birth to first sale," he tells his wife.

"We'd love to hear more about log books and the Remington bronze," says Lola, "but the *Jimmys* that were swimming in the bay last night are piled high and ready for consumption. So log off, and that's an order."

When Mark returns to the breakfast room, he finds Sara and five-year old Jamie touching the horse. "I can't be certain but my instincts tell me that it's the real McCoy," he boasts. "I'll have to see if there's an alpha-numeric code stamped on the base, which is the edition number. Nevertheless, it only cost me $800 since the saleslady thought it was a recast made in China."

"It seems too good to be true," says Sara. "Even if it's a recast, it would cost that much to reproduce it, except in China where their workers are paid one-tenth of what American workers get for their labor."

On the following Monday at 11:00 AM, Mark is typing memos on the computer inside his office on the second floor of Bethlehem Steel at Sparrows Point when his secretary, Miss Virginia 'Ginny' Potts, informs him of a call from a lady at Women in Need Thrift Store on Howard Street. "Put her through, Miss Potts," says Mark, using the cursor to turn a page of the weekly planner with his right hand and reaching for the phone with his left. "This is Mark Hopkins. I'm surprised to hear from you. Did my check bounce?"

"This is Miss Turtledove, the lady who sold you the Remington bronze on Saturday at WIN. No, your check didn't bounce. However, we have a problem with the sale, and I'd like to put the owner of the bronze and donor of the proceeds on the line to explain everything better than I could."

"Put him on, please."

"My name is Al Rhodes, but everyone calls me Dusty."

"I've heard of the name 'Dusty Rhodes,'" says Mark. "Wasn't he the Lieutenant-Commander who designed the insignia for the Blue Angels?"

"Yes, he is my father, but let's gets down to business. When I donated the Remington bronze to WIN, I left two conditions before it could be sold. They were not to sell it for less than $800."

"Yes, that's what Miss Turtledove told me on Saturday."

"But the other condition was that they should check it out first before selling it. That means calling in an expert in Remington bronzes to appraise it and determine if it's worth more than $800. I intend to donate it to WIN and take the donation off my taxes, so I need written proof of its value for the IRS. WIN did not fully follow my instructions and I will not sign a consignor's release until both conditions are satisfied."

"I tend to agree with you, although money was transferred from buyer, me, to seller, WIN, as your agent, which constitutes a valid sale. Also, asking someone to check it out is an ambiguous condition. You should have been more specific when you dropped it off at WIN. However, I consider myself a fair man and am willing to bargain with you. Perhaps you would consider an idea that suddenly popped into my head."

"I'm listening," says Dusty.

"I'll contact Sotheby's or Christie's in New York and arrange for an expert in the field of Remington bronzes to examine it. I'll even pay for their appraisal, provided you agree to sell it to me for 50 percent of their appraised value. You might call it 'splitting the difference' in a resale to me. "

"Can you run that by me again?"

"If you were to consign the Remington bronze to Sotheby's or Christie's in New York for one of their major sales of American art, you, as a consignor, would probably pay the auction house a commission of 20 percent when it's sold, plus additional charges for packing and shipping, storage, insurance, color illustration in the catalog, and God knows what else. Now, if we cannot come to an agreement, we'll both probably turn the matter over to our attorneys, so you can add more costs. It seems that the matter could be settled out of court if you're willing to take 50 percent of the fair market value to be determined by a reputable appraiser in bronzes."

"Miss Turtledove at WIN thought it might be a bronze produced in China. I'm not ready to concede such a notion from a saleslady who doesn't know what she is talking about," says Dusty. "Consequently, I will abide by your decision to have Sotheby's or Christie's determine its value. How long do you expect it will take before you'll get their appraisal?"

"Two weeks seems reasonable, provided an expert is available," Mark answers. "In the meantime, you have my word that the bronze won't be out of my hands, except for examination by the expert in Remington bronzes."

After hanging up the telephone, Mark says to himself, "I knew it was too good to be true."

After telephoning Sotheby's main office in New York, he is informed that their expert is already in Washington DC as part of a free appraisal-day promotion on Wednesday. If Mark can manage to take it there, the expert will examine it free of charge and give a verbal opinion as to its fair market value. If the owner wants a written appraisal for donation purposes, a small fee would be required.

The timing is perfect for both parties and Mark arranges his schedule to drive to the Ritz Carlton in Washington DC. As he walks through the lobby everyone pauses to watch this six-foot four inch handsome man, dressed casually in a Ravens jacket, carrying something under a pink bathrobe. Hardly anyone would know it's a Remington bronze titled 'Broncho Buster', weighing at least 35 pounds and measuring 23 ½-inches high.

An hour later Mark is driving on the expressway back to Baltimore, smiling and gloating that his hunch about the Remington bronze being a genuine cast by Henry-Bonnard in 1895 may be another score. "But how could I have missed not seeing the cast number stamped next to the foundry marking?" he asks himself several times. "Fifty thousand dollars, the fair market value placed on it by the Sotheby's expert, is something that I did not anticipate. That means I have to pay either Dusty or WIN an additional $25,000. Well, no matter, it's for a good cause and the title of ownership of the bronze will be mine. I'll be able to look at Remington's *Broncho Buster* every day and pat myself on the back for recognizing quality when I see it."

On Thursday morning Mark telephones Dusty and gives him an update on the value of the Remington bronze. "Although I don't have the paperwork yet from Sotheby's, a cashier's check for $25,000 could be delivered to WIN this morning, provided you sign an agreement, which is attached to my check, withdrawing any further claims to my legal right to own the Remington bronze."

"If you have no objections, I'd like to see you in person, sign the agreement and deliver the check personally to WIN," says Dusty.

"That's fine with me," says Mark. "Meet me at my office around 1:00 PM."

At that precise time, after Dusty is handed a check made payable to 'WIN', Mark asks him if he wouldn't mind telling him how he acquired the bronze in the first place.

"Are you sure you want to know the story? Because much of it is just a story and may not have any validity."

"Lay it on me, Dusty," says Mark.

"I won it in a poker game," says Dusty.

"You what?"

"Four of us were playing poker and the pot was about $2,000 when I raised the stakes $800 against an airline pilot sitting across from me. It was a scene right out of 'The Cincinnati Kid.' I'm getting nervous just telling you about it."

"Would you like a sedative to relax your nerves?"

"No, I just need a moment to clear up my nasal passages," says Dusty, blowing his nose into his bare hands then inhaling from a medicated inhaler. By the way, where's your john?"

After returning to Mark's office and looking refreshed, Dusty continues with his explanation. "When I raised him $800, the pilot said he didn't have any cash left and offered to put in the pot a Remington bronze that he brought back from Rome."

"Incredible," says Mark, wiping his brow.

"When I confessed that I knew nothing about bronzes, much less the works of Frederic Remington," says Dusty, "he said he found it on a doorstep of an antiques shop along the Via Veneto in Rome. It was being used as a doorstop to keep the front door open. The owner said he knew nothing about it except that someone gave it to him on consignment for $800 but kept the nameplate that read 'Presented to Enrico Caruso by the Sons of the Italian-American Club of New York.' That's the story in a nutshell. I won the poker hand, including the bronze, which represented $800 of my total winnings."

"Dusty, that's one helluva story, whether or not it's true," says Mark. "I'm almost as ecstatic as hearing from one of my SEALS that everyone returned safely after a dangerous mission. "I'll title it 'From a Doorstop in Rome to a Place of Honor in Baltimore.' Your story is good enough for part of a movie under development at Ridgefield Studios."

Chapter 4

On the first day of June at Ridgefield, emotions take a rollercoaster ride at the breakfast table after Abigail offers a short prayer and stands up to say, "Today is filled with many surprises that will soon unfold before your very eyes. Our founder, Mark Hopkins, unexpectedly dropped by to see if we're still here and continuing to do what he expected us to do after he retired from Ridgefield. By the way, Mark, remind me to give you a letter from Sotheby's that was delivered yesterday afternoon. But here's breathtaking news that comes from China."

"Don't tell me they want to buy our *ebouys*?" asks Kim, with some trepidation. "I knew that sooner or later someone would wake up and see the benefits of our *ebuoy*."

"A good guess, but not the correct guess," says Abigail. "The Chinese Government has agreed to purchase the film rights to 'Greta's Ludicrous Tent' for $5,000,000. They view it as a documentary and propaganda vehicle to illustrate the success of the Wew twins, whose mother was born in China. Everyone who contributed to the film will find a bonus in their Christmas stocking. Even though he is CEO Emeritus, Mark recommended that the money be used as a springboard for a sequel, so get your ideas to Kim Bozzetti and Sergio Leone, who will be spearheading the film project again."

"That calls for a celebration," Kim and Sergio say in unison. After being closely linked romantically for a year, they are beginning to think and speak as one person. Their collaboration has more than a touch of romance, for they are almost inseparable during the day and night.

"I'd like to have half of the money for James (Wong Howe Jr.) to buy a *Panascan* camera," says Sergio, who heads up the film unit at Ridgefield.

"And I'd like to have the other half to hire a screenwriter with Academy-Award credentials," says Kim who oversees all projects related to film in addition to heading up the R&D Lab.

"Keep your seats and money-grabbing thoughts to yourself," says Abigail, laughing, "at least for the next few minutes because I'm just getting started. Get ready for the next round -- and I'm not talking about Gaby's crepes! Rumors have been flying around Ridgefield faster than flies around a cow pasture; especially those about my retirement from Ridgefield LLC, which are true. I'm getting better at announcing my departure. The first time was five years ago, when I retired as director of the museum in Hagerstown. Our board of directors has accepted my resignation with regret, and gave me a solid-gold watch with their sentiments engraved on the inside case. I'll stay another three months, until Labor Day, and hope a successor will be installed by then. I'd like to promote someone within the organization to take my place. Ridgefield LLC has many talented people in its organization, which means my decision will be a very difficult one."

Everyone is ecstatic to hear about the success success of Ridgefield's sale of its film to the Chinese Government but stunned and disappointed about the unexpected resignation of Abigail, a co-founder of Ridgefield.

"What'll we do without you running this place?" Womble says to Abigail. "You made this place tick better than a Patek Philippe watch. This is a shocking moment that takes my breath away."

Womble quickly assimilates in his mind the idea of him being the logical choice to succeed Abigail since he was her right-hand man. If selected by Mark, he would be forced to pass most of his work involving intellectual properties to his partner and lover, Eloise. Both talk about marriage but, at their age, are afraid to take the plunge. Decisions involving matrimony are often difficult for those reaching 45, age-wise, not waist or bust-wise.

"What are your plans and where will you live?" asks Liz.

"I'll be moving back to my condo in Baltimore and plan to write a book or two," says Abigail. "If I don't get busy with it soon, it will never get published."

"Speaking of getting busy," says Kim, "you can take my name *outta* the hat for consideration as your successor. I am too involved in the development of our *ebuoys* and their deployment in the Bay. I can't do both jobs and heavily depend on Liz for her technical expertise in the design of the *ebouy's* computer wizard. Liz and I are a team that Mark had in mind for deployment in the Chesapeake Bay and Patapsco River, especially along the shoreline of Bethlehem Steel at Sparrows Point."

"Kim is right on the money," Liz says, popping out of her seat. "The electronic sensors inside each *ebouy* and its technology can be applied wherever needed to detect the presence of contaminants. We've heard rumors of neighbors who have complained of contaminated drinking water and bad odors. Therefore, kindly remove my name from consideration."

York rises out of his seat, pauses to give everyone a broad smile and says, "If I had a hat, I'd throw it in the ring for Abigail's successor. Sandy and I have loved our time and work here immensely and want to see Ridgefield continue on its path to serve Red Cross Vets as its first priority --correction –along with our science projects to detect pollutants, of course."

"Although this is all news to me," says Sandy, "I'll go along with whatever my husband decides is best for everyone concerned."

Greta waits until last and gushes, "I have a secret that I've been waiting to share with you and now is the right time. I'm moving up in the world of broadcasting and next month you will see me on television. I'll talk about your horoscope and team up with Henny Youngster, a marriage counselor for Kent County who gave advice on "Love and Other Disorders of the Heart" on our radio broadcasts two years ago. He gave up his marriage counseling job because no one paid heed to his advice, went back to college and graduated with a degree in meteorology. He will join me as a 'good-humor' weatherman and tell a quick story of human behavior affected by the weather. The broadcast will air on the Discovery Channel."

"This is turning into an incredible breakfast briefing," says Abigail. "There must definitely be something in Gaby's crepes, akin to Performance Enhancement Drugs (PED) that are responsible for so many changes going on around Ridgefield. And we haven't even begun to talk about the development of Swan Haven Marina yet."

After breakfast, Abigail motions for Mark to meet her inside his old office. She hands him an envelope and says, "It's from Sotheby's in New York. Somehow they must have had your old address in their files. If you reply, remember to give them your new address in Baltimore."

After reading it, Mark tells her, "It's the appraisal of a Remington bronze that I bought at WIN on Howard Street. I'd like you to see it whenever you can find the time to visit us at Cylburn. It is a remarkable work by a man better known for his paintings of the Old West, but someday his reputation as an artist may be surpassed by his work as a sculptor."

When Kim mentioned earlier at breakfast that she is 'too involved,' she also meant her involvement with Sergio. Later this night at the stroke of midnight, he tells her, "I've known you for a year and that's enough foreplay already. I want to settle down and want you for my wife."

"I've loved you from the first moment I met you," says Kim. "I accept your proposal."

After embracing, they pull down the sheets of their queen-size bed in one of the custom-built trailers near the main house, and do what most lovers do at this point in their lives: make love; for Italians, it's *appassionato amore.*

On the first of July, the Discovery Channel introduces a new segment, sponsored by AARP, called "Fifteen Minutes with Henny and Greta." The broadcast is *live* at noon and fed to subscribers in high-definition, emanating from a studio inside the R&L Building of Ridgefield Farms.

Henny Youngster, a handsome and debonair 40-year old, is anxious to open his segment with up-to-the-minute weather news. Using the latest satellite technology and tie-ins with the National Weather Bureau, he takes a position beside a 40-inch diagonal touchscreen telestrator, with state-of-the-art digital technology, and gets ready to discuss weather patterns in real time.

"Did you hear my last warm-up?" Henny asks Carolyn Presutti, the floor director who motions with her hands that it's one minute to go *live.*

Before she can answer him, a cameraman whispers, "I certainly hope so."

"It is 90 degrees in the nation's capital and love is in the air despite the feuds between congressmen and women," says Henny, gushing to begin his segment. "Our DC birdwatcher called from her secluded spot along the row of the cherry blossoms on the Washington mall and said she overheard an elderly wife ask her husband sitting beside her on a park bench, 'Do you see that couple over there kissing so passionately? Why don't you do like that man?' to which he replied, 'I will when I know her better.'"

Henny glances at his telestrator and continues, "Rain is expected for Salisbury this afternoon, so all sporting events outside were cancelled because the teams did not want to pay in *clement* weather. As for Anchorage, a cold snap from the Artic has turned the roads into icy corridors. *Un zo* for you brazen drivers, keep both hands on the steering wheel and don't scream like the passengers in the car you're driving. And finally, the murderer who was supposed to get a lethal injection at noon was granted a brief reprieve. A tornado came across Arkansas, preventing the delivery of sterile needles."

Greta, in the meantime, is applying some makeup and fidgeting at her computer monitor. "I can't do much with this face except use some powder to take the shine off my big *schnozzle*," she says to Carolyn.

"Your hair is perfect and the styling makes you look 21 again," says Carolyn, an attractive, charismatic 32-year old brunette. She auditioned for the co-host job but lost out when Mark lobbied the producers on Greta's behalf. "My time will come if she ever falls flat on her face and says something offensive or provocative," she says under her breath.

A few minutes later Carolyn begins a countdown to Greta's portion of the newscast. "This is Greta 'Bow-Wow' Howl," she says, smiling broadly, "ready and willing to answer questions from callers who are facing a dilemma in their lives and want to know their horoscope."

"I'm ninety and calling from Baltimore," says the first caller, "and would like to know: When will the Orioles make the playoffs?"

"Once in a blue moon!" says Greta. "But during a commercial break, I can feed some data into 'Dazzling Dave,' an IBM Univac computer from the 1950's. Dave will digest their record of 14 consecutive losing seasons, batting statistics of all hitters on their current roster, innings pitched and strikeout-to-walk ratios by their pitching staff. But data such as their ability to advance runners in scoring positions along with factors such as heart and passion to play hard every game are intangibles and difficult to measure. They make Dave hiccup or fart. In the meantime have a *National Boh*, one of our sponsors. And for seniors like you, here's more encouraging news from another one of our sponsors, AARP."

A commercial publicizing their health plan begins running across the screen as Greta transfers the data from the Baseball Digest into a small machine on her desk that resembles a crystal ball, with a visor window on one side. A second later an IBM card with punch holes pops out like a ticket to a movie theatre. She immediately turns ninety degrees in her swivel chair and inserts it into 'Dazzling Dave.' The machine begins to roar like the wheels of a locomotive. A few seconds later, punch cards fly out at lightning speed into ten slots on the side of the machine. An old carnival organ grinder toots five times and the computer stops wheezing and panting for breath as Greta removes the lone card from the tenth slot.

"If I remember your question correctly," she says, swinging her chair around and leaning her head until it bounces off the microphone, "you asked: 'When will the Orioles make the playoffs?' According to 'Dazzling Dave,' the answer is: 'On the next eclipse of the sun.' But don't be disheartened. Dave said that there's always light at the end of the tunnel, a pot of gold at the end of the rainbow, a bird in the hand is worth more than two in the bush leagues, whatever all that means."

"Sorry to interrupt, Greta," says Henny, "but how do you know so much about baseball?"

"Growing up as a tomboy on the Eastern Shore, I was a scorekeeper and played around with a lot of ball players," she says facetiously.

The floor director motions that she has an additional two minutes before the next commercial.

"OK, we'll take our next caller, who goes by name of Axelrod. He wasn't supposed to tell me his name. I'll call him Axel for short. Proceed with your question."

"I'm in love," says Axel, "and I'm thinking about proposing to my girlfriend who lives next door. Do you think her father would approve of me as a husband for his only daughter?"

"Stop worrying about the father and start worrying about your girlfriend," says Greta. "She's the one you have to satisfy. If you get married, where will you live?"

"In my parent's home to make ends meet until we can save up and get a place of our own," he answers.

"Where do you work?" asks Greta.

"We're unemployed like so many millions of Americans who can't find a job, but we pick up some loose change running errands, especially for our parents."

"Are they big tippers?"

"No," answers Axel.

"Well, based on everything you've told me, the alignment of the stars and planets say: 'love, *true* love is the most important ingredient in getting married.' But I have one more question to ask you, if you don't mind my getting personal," says Greta.

"Shoot," says Axel. "I have nothing to hide."

"Have you given any thought about what will happen if you have a baby?"

"Well, we've been lucky so far," Axel says assuredly.

"By the way, you didn't tell me how old you are," Greta says, becoming more inquisitive.

"We're both fourteen!" Axel boasts.

Greta leans forward and presses the cough button on the console to prevent her voice from being heard and exclaims, "You little turd. You need a good whipping and must write a thousand times on the black board, 'I'll be nice to my girlfriend but keep my pecker in my pants!"

"Oh my," says Brian at the top of his voice, "here's a late-breaking bulletin coming in about a hurricane moving at 200 miles an hour off the coast of the Virgin Islands, which could be over the Chesapeake Bay by tomorrow night. So batten down the hatches and prepare for the worst."

"Speaking of late-breaking news bulletins," says Greta, "It's nice to end our broadcast with a reading of your horoscope, based on the angle of the Earth's axis and alignment with the stars and planets:

For *Aries*, March 21 to April 19: Did you get outta that hole you recently fell in? Don't look for anyone to help because they're too busy *jerking off* to care about helping anyone at this moment. In times of crisis, always remember: 'You're on your own, kid.'

For *Taurus*, April 20 to May 20: No time for *back-slapping* to win a friend. Don't wait for the next shoe to drop; it may have a foot attached to it and kick you in the rear end. Put your energy and eagerness to work for your family. After all, *they* should come first.

For *Gemini*, May 22 to June 20: Get those fears and fleas off your back, the ones looking for a free ride at your expense. Even fears and fleas can weigh you down.

For *Cancer*, June 21 to July 21: You are destined for greatness since researchers are making advances in the fight against mediocrity. You've walked the walk and talked the talk long enough now. Your future is bright, at least for the next 24 hours.

For *Leo*, July 22 to August 22: Now is the time for you to roar like a Lion king but try not to scare anyone by exposing too much of your teeth. And be ready to take some action after roaring. Any action is a good thing, even if it's bad because we learn from our mistakes.

For *Virgo*, August 23 to September 22: No more petting and foreplay for you. It's time to grab your lover and make love until it hurts. Think as if you were a Bluefin crab who can make love for two days and never brag about it.

For *Libra*, September 23 to October 22: By now you should be in sync with your life's partner, so get them to do the work you would be doing yourself.

For *Scorpio*, October 23 to November 21: You are glowing, but don't overdo it and blow a fuse.

For *Sagittarius*, November 22 to December 21: Of course, you can be better than you are, but you have to put words into actions. Those speak louder than words.

For *Capricorn*, December 22 to January 20: At long last you've discovered that not only are you not the center of the universe, you're not even the center of attention. But your confidence is important and it will lift you to new heights. Behave and continue to believe in yourself.

For *Aquarius*, January 21 to February 19: If you're thinking about moving to a new neighborhood with better schools for your children, go for it. It can't be worse than the spot you're in now.

Finally, for *Pisces*, February 20 to March 20: *Pisces* make the best lovers in water or on land. But love alone won't do it in today's money-mad world. Take a course in a new field. Now is the time to re-educate yourself."

The floor director motions with her hands that only 20 seconds remain. "That's the long and short of it," says Greta, "planet-wise. And now my final philosophical advice of the day is: Give yourself a little space so you be a better listener. Here's an example: Let's say that you're dreaming and in that dream you see a man that resembles one of Jesus' disciples and you ask him: 'Are you one of God's disciples and were you at the crucifixion of Jesus Christ?' After a reasonable pause, he answers, 'Oh boy'. How do you interpret his answer?"

Greta moves her plastic candy-cane-colored spectacles without lens to the top of her head and leans forward to the camera and says "Now, think and interpret for a moment. Did he answer slowly with compassion and an inflection downward, such as 'oh…boy', as if he suddenly felt pain in his heart…or did he answer quickly with joy and an inflection upward such as 'oh boy'? Do you see how difficult it is to listen and interpret something as simple as these two words?"

Brian leans his head into the picture going out live over the network and asks, "Can you give me another example, please?"

Off the top of my head, I can't, so let's save that question for our next show," says Greta, spinning her swivel chair around and grinning like a cat that just swallowed a mouse.

Another 30-second commercial, sponsored by AARP, reminds viewers of the benefits of taking their flu shots. After the commercial ends, Carolyn smiles as she hears in her earphones 'that's a wrap' and gives Greta a thumbs-up sign. "You may have thought it was good," says Greta. "The proof of the pudding will be if Discovery Channel and people watching liked it."

When her segment is over, Little Ben Bender meets her in the lobby of the station and asks, "Are you surprised to see me waiting for you?"

"More than surprised. More like pleased."

"There's something that I've wanted to talk over with you," says Little Ben. "If you have no objections, I'll drive you home."

The conversation is lighthearted as Little Ben drives out of Ridgefield Farm. But he turns his car to the right instead of left onto Eastern Neck Road. "This is not the way to my house," says Greta. "Why are we heading towards the Wildlife Refuge?"

"You'll have the answer in due time."

Three miles later they pass the entrance to the Refuge, with Little Ben smiling all the way. "Now I am getting curious," says Greta.

Little Ben pulls over to the shoulder on the right and rushes around the car to open her door. They walk hand-in-hand through a short section of the woods fronting Eastern Neck Road until they reach a clearing. A chorus of songbirds -- a Robin, Chickadee, Cardinal, Rose-Breasted Grosbeak, Sparrow and Finch -- all begin chirping at the top of their lungs. In the still air of July 1st, it sounds like the Mormon Tabernacle Choir.

Little Ben lifts her onto a tree stump and says, "You deserve to be put on a pedestal." Then he gets down on one knee and hands her a jewel box with an engagement ring inside. Tears form in her eyes as Little Ben makes a marriage proposal. A farm boy like him cannot be expected to mouth the words as if he were William Shakespeare; although somewhat awkwardly pronounced, they are well-meaning and from his heart.

After a long pause and a kiss, Greta tells him, "We're both 45 and set in our ways, which doesn't mean we can't compromise and come to an understanding later. It's just not the time for me to take on more responsibility. I'm still trying to fight my way to the top in a man's world."

"I'd like to help you make it to the top," says Ben, "and give you the support you'll need to stay there."

"That's reassuring," says Greta, giving him a kiss on his lips. "For now, I would like us to be good friends, best friends."

Tears begin to form in Little Ben's eyes. Rejection was not what he expected and is difficult for him to accept. For the next few days, when he recalls her rejection of his proposal, he tells himself, "I've set my direction-finder on Greta and mean to have her. I simply must find a different and better tack for my sails. As long as I stay focused, maybe tomorrow will bring a change in the winds of her mind."

Chapter 5

On the Fourth of July, Roland N. Cash, one of the twin Vets on R&R at Ridgefield, drives his car into a small parking lot adjacent to Bethlehem Steel at Sparrows Point. It's on a parcel of land fronting the Patapsco River and a few miles from the Inner Harbor of Baltimore. Signs around the parking lot read: 'Parking permitted only for guests of the Institute. Visitors not allowed on the premises. Call the Institute for more information.'

As he locks his car, he hears the sound of firecrackers going off. After checking to make sure no explosions are coming from his car, he spots the entrance to a fort or stockade with its huge sign that reads: "Institute for the Very Well Endowed." He realizes the sound of fireworks is coming from over that sign.

The stockade is a throwback to colonial days. Twelve-foot high walls are built of vertical tree trunks stripped of their bark and closely aligned, completely encircling the fort. Peering down is a guard, a retired forest ranger with the eyesight of a bald eagle, to see who's prowling around the walls of the fort. In olden days when a guard saw the fort was under attack by Indians, he would fire his shotgun into the air. Nowadays, he watches the GPS screen on his cell that gives him the location of anyone approaching the perimeter and, using the keypad on his iPhone, presses an electronic alarm that would scare the pants off any prowlers. He can issue a warning to any invaders, especially paparazzi who try to take a picture of nude patients with their telephoto lens and sell it to the highest bidder over the Internet. The Institute intended to install a wire around the fort to give invaders an electric shock, but it was considered 'inhumane' by the zoning board, so the Institute settled for a series of motion detectors.

The ranger asks him, "State your name and business or be on your way. This is private property and no one is admitted without an appointment."

"My name is Roland N. Cash and I have an appointment to see Dr. Froid."

"This is *wanger Wobin Woberts,*" he speaks into his cell. "Mister *Woland* is here to see Dr. Fwoid. Claims he has an appointment."

"The first name is 'Roland,' not *Woland,*" he tells the guard.

"That's what I said, *'Woland,'*" he says, pressing the automatic door opener on a keypad. "And remember, everyone must sign in at the *wegistration* desk."

After Roland is admitted inside the main building, the first thing he notices is a plaque on the right wall of a short foyer that reads: "The Institute was designed by Disciples of Frank Lloyd Wright to meet the Arts and Crafts standards established by the County Planning Commission. The walls of the fort were all constructed by the labor of local politicians as punishment for spending more than they should have and for forcing Baltimore County citizens into a double-dip recession. No smoking or drinking is permitted on the premises.' On the left wall is a small sign, printed in 12-point font that reads: 'If you can read these words, you don't need glasses.'

In the center of a large reception room is a circular counter, manned – correction -- womaned by a sexy long-haired five foot receptionist. Her face peers above the countertop.

"I didn't realize security was so tight around here," says Roland.

"You'd be amazed at the type of people who want to take a photo of what's going on around the swimming pool and miniature golf course," she tells him. "When the Institute opened a year ago, the neighbors had problems getting into their driveways because of the overflow from our parking lot. Then the neighbors started to look through the holes in the fence and complained to the police department about a nudist colony in their neighborhood. Finally the BCPD set up an automated recording that answered their complaints with: 'Our menu has recently changed. Press one for complaints about the Institute. If you're calling about the 'nudity run rampant,' please be advised that we are seriously looking into it.'"

"Would you mind holding off on the history of the Institute and let me meet Dr. Froid as soon as possible?"

"Sorry, I didn't know you were in a big hurry this morning," she tells him. "His office is to my left, the door with italic lettering."

After opening the door, he sees a beautiful 24-year old brunette sitting behind her desk and wearing a see-through negligee. She leans toward the intercom and says, "Dr. Froid, this is Miss Affectionado," then sneezes twice.

Rolland takes two tissues from a box of Kleenex on her desk and hands them to her.

"Gesundheit," says Dr. Froid, over the intercom. "You better take care of that cold before it spreads throughout the entire camp. That reminds me, where do members hide a Kleenex when they need it?"

"I'll get right on it, doctor. As soon as you finish with this next patient, I'm going home to crawl into bed with a *hot toddy*."

"Ah, if I were 25 again, I'd ask permission to join you so there would be two *hot toddies*, ah bodies, under the covers," says Dr. Froid.

"In the meantime here's a referral from Cambridge."

"From Harvard, my alma mater?" he asks.

"No, from the VA Clinic in Cambridge, Maryland. He's anxious to see you and says he has a serious problem."

"Oh my, hold all calls and send him in, please," he says, swallowing the last half of a Swedish creampuff overloaded with so much cream it almost completely coats his moustache.

"You can go in, Mr. Cash."

Dr. Froid is dressed in his long-sleeved, heavily starched physician's scrub with a fiberglass replica of a gold crown from the Middle Ages tilted to one side of his head and shakes Roland's hand at the door, leaving cream on his hands, too. "My secretary said that this is an emergency," says Dr. Froid. "It better be one because I am fully booked today and must keep everything *smowing floothly*, ah flowing smoothly."

Dr. Froid, who's not only near-sighted but very short-sighted as well, leads Roland slowly over to a comfortable chair beside his desk. "Damned arthritis will force me to retire next year when I hit 77, my lucky number," he says, moving his spectacles to tip of his nose and picking up from his desk an 8-inch wide magnifying glass. When he gets a closer look at Roland, Dr. Froid realizes that he's wearing only a jock strap and a goose is sitting on his head, and asks, "Now, just relax and tell me what your problem is?"

"The goose says, 'Hey Doc, can you lend me a hand and get this guy off my ass?"

"Are you shitting me?" Dr. Froid blurts out so strongly that his crown shifts to one side of his head. "Shoo, shush, damn it! Get the hell outta my office and go back to Canada where you belong. I don't see anyone without an appointment with Miss Affectionado."

Dr. Froid and Roland team up and manage to get the goose to fly out a window. However, before leaving the goose looks at all the nude photos on the walls and statues of nude women sitting on pedestals in the corners of his office and says to them, "I am getting a bit queer and feel an erection coming on. It must be time to get back to the Refuge and relieve myself of these lustful *wabbits*, ah habits, too."

After catching his breath, Dr. Froid checks his heartbeat with a stethoscope hanging around his neck then sits on the edge of his desk and asks, "Now, my good man, what's all the fuss about an emergency? Your heartbeat is as strong as an ox."

"Dr. Froid, I want to tell you about me and my brother," says Roland. "We got this problem of chasing women with big tits. The doctor at the VA clinic in Cambridge thought, spending a therapy session or two with you and seeing all these beautiful women would prove that bosoms are not as important as a good, healthy mind."

"A cure is not as simple as one or two therapy sessions at the Institute. Seeing is not believing and not a cure unto itself; seeing won't get those lustful *wabbits* out of your psyche."

"Do you mean 'rabbits' or 'habits'?"

"I'm referring to anything running around inside your brain. As you know, we are strictly a research center for the study of human behavior of the well-endowed."

"What precisely does 'well-endowed' mean, Herr Professor?"

"It means men with big bank accounts and women with big breasts. However, character does enter into the equation when someone's chasing after women. But how do we know one or two of you won't misbehave here?"

"We'll give you our word of honor; after all, we were good soldiers before we landed in Iraq. You can trust us."

"I'll only allow you both on the premises if each wears an electronic ankle bracelet to monitor your whereabouts."

"That's more than fair, Doc," says Roland, shaking his hand vigorously.

"Let me ask you another question, please. How often do you think about sex during the day and do you have dreams about lust at night?"

"I'll answer your last question first, if you don't mind. You can have dreams only at night. I never *hoyd* of anyone having dreams during the day although my teacher, Miss Hufnagle at Patterson High, always scolded me for daydreaming in her class."

Dr. Froid looks at his registration card and says, "You're on R&R at the Refuge in Ridgefield?"

"That's right, Doc."

"How in the world did you land there?"

"My brother and I were paratroopers, bailing out of planes at 10,000 feet over the desert about 100 miles outside of Baghdad when our parachutes got tangled and we landed on our heads."

"That must have been a shocking development."

"Shocking *ain't* the word for it, Doc," says Roland. "When we woke up, we were in a Red Cross hangar, being attended to by a core of sexy military nurses with big bosoms. They sure took good care of all our pain and suffering. Since that moment, all we ever thought of was being around women with big ..."

"Yes, I am getting a clearer picture of the origin of your syndrome," says Dr. Froid.

"We decided to take a medical leave of absence and applied to Ridgefield because they have a quiet wildlife refuge next to their R&R lodge, which is only two hours away from the VA clinic in Cambridge where we are being evaluated. I think that's it in a nutshell, Doc."

"Very interesting and most perceptive," says Dr. Froid. "I can see you have a keen mind inside your bald head."

"Bald head? Oh shit, what happened to my *toup*?"

"Are you sure you were wearing a toupee?"

"Are you shitting me? Of course I had a *toup*. I bet that fuckin' goose flew off with it. By the way, I *hoyd* a rumor that you're thinking of installing a Ferris wheel inside the fort, ah, institute."

"It seems to work in Stockholm, so we're thinking of giving it a try to make our little world go around at *Sparris* Point," says Dr. Froid, pausing to straighten the crown on his head. "Does your brother share the same sexual urges and fascination for women's bosoms that you have?"

"The same, more or less," says Roland, sighing.

"Perhaps since you're twins, you have a syndrome called 'Hypersexual Disorder', referred to as HD. It may be caused by medications that you're taking. We'll run some tests and if they come back 'positive', anti-depressants or inhibitor drugs will do the trick."

"You mean it?" asks Roland, pronouncing it slowly to imitate one of his favorite actors, Gary Cooper. "Anything else you want to ask me?"

"As a matter of fact, I'd like to ask: If you could be one person in the world for 24 hours, who would you be?"

"That's a tough question. I know it wouldn't be the President of the United States."

"Why is that?"

"Can you imagine if a photographer caught the *Prez* inside the Institute, chasing those beautiful dolls with big ...?"

"I get the point," says Dr. Froid, interrupting him before he can complete his answer. "Perhaps you should consider taking a warm bath with a dash of bleach instead of mineral salts."

"Would that tone down our anxiety about chasing women?"

"Frankly, it's on a case-by-case basis, but it'll surely brighten your skin," Dr. Froid says, pushing him out the door and handing him a slip to see Miss Affectionado for a follow-up appointment.

Roland reads it quickly and hands it to her, saying, "Dr. Froid has given his authorization for a follow-up session."

"Ah, yes, I see that he wrote, 'Approved for an erection.'"

"Szowee!" says Roland.

"Not so fast, Roland," she says. "He probably means approved for an 'injection.' Doc has a lot on his mind and should have retired five years ago."

Before leaving her office, Roland reads another sign posted over a doorway to the pool: "Anyone walking outside enters an unsafe zone. Proceed at your own risk. Only hats and wigs are permitted to shade the sun. Check your Desperately Needed Articles (DNA) here; tipping is encouraged." At the last minute, when the receptionist is not looking, Roland ducks outside and hides behind a couple relaxing in their lounge chairs. "Suddenly the devil in me said to eavesdrop on them to learn more about this place."

"It was nice of you to accept my invitation to meet here on a blind date," says Johnny 'Jon' Weissmuller, a handsome young man in his early 30's.

"It was courageous of you to make such proposal," says Maureen 'Mo' O'Hara, his gorgeous, statuesque 25-year old date. "I hardly recognize you with your clothes off."

"I wonder if anyone met here, fell in love and got married. I know that when Cupid sends his arrows in your direction, the heart takes control of your mind. Later on, people can learn about each other as they go along."

"I wouldn't fall in love unless I knew everything about a person there was to know *before* taking those vows."

"That makes good sense," says Jon, who rises from his chair, climbs to the 10-meter springboard facing the pool and does a perfect forward 4 ½-sommersault dive in the Tuck position.

"Very impressive; you executed that like an Olympian."

"I was a runner-up on the Olympic team," says Jon. "You see, I told you, people can learn about each other as they go along."

Mo, wanting to impress him, too, dives into the pool and does 50 continuous laps back and forth across the Olympic pool.

"That was incredible," says Jon, handing her a towel to dry herself off. "Were you a Navy SEAL?"

"No," says Mo, hardly out of breath. "I was a call girl in Chestertown and worked both sides of the Chester River!"

After Roland overhears her exclamation, he snakes his way out of the premises and says, "*Szowlwee.* I can't wait to get back for my next appointment."

Chapter 6

Meanwhile, it is noon inside the kitchenette of her home in Rock Hall as Bonnie Bratcher Floyd begins feeding her four year old son, fathered by Bud Wayne, and her two year old son, fathered by her husband, Pretty Boy Floyd. Whenever they're sitting in their highchairs, they know it's time for their mother to teach them a few new words and sounds along with the nutritious food formulated especially for them.

An hour later she hears something that sounds like a car backfiring and continues reading a book to her children. She soon notices that they are a little drowsy and carries them to her bedroom. "It's time to see if any soft crabs are sloughing in the tanks and check up on my big baby, Pretty Boy," she tells herself.

After walking across a short driveway behind her house, she enters the sloughing shed and finds her husband sitting in his wheelchair with his head leaning into one of the sloughing tanks. The red color of the water tells her everything she needs to know: he has ended his life. She grabs her cell and phones 911.

Twenty minutes later, the rescue squad of the Rock Hall Fire Department carries his body out of the sloughing shed. Before the driver opens the door to his vehicle, he hands a Bible to Bonnie and tells her, "This was held between his legs."

When Bonnie opens it, she reads the following note in her husband's handwriting:

"For those who find me dead, what do you see?
What are you thinking as you look at me?
The pretty face of a man, who espoused to be,
Never satisfied, a bit loony who became a roving honeybee?
I tried to make the best of each day as it unfolds,
Taking nothing seriously except yearly winter colds,
I'll tell you more about myself and I'm not bragging,
I thank God for giving me a wife never nagging,
She accepted my faults, weaknesses and tragic mishap,
And cared for me when the devil put booze and coke in my lap,
Mostly I'll miss holding our son on my knee,
And hope someone will tell him what misplaced talent could be,
I shudder to think of the future ahead,
And therefore take the easy way out with a bullet through my head."

"I knew he was distraught and depressed with the increasing pain to his back, but thought his medication was working so he could feel productive in our soft-crab business," she tells a policeman. "He should have complained more to the doctor for stronger anti-depressives. It may have helped; maybe not. Being a paraplegic can be devastating, especially when hope of recovery is fleeting. He never could get over the fact that he killed a beautiful woman by driving under the influence of booze and coke."

A month later, the twin Vets, Roland and Cary Cash, are pleased with their sessions at the Institute and have decided to look for an investment or business opportunity in Rock Hall and settle down there. They hear through the grapevine that Bonnie Bratcher Floyd is thinking of closing her sloughing shed since she collected $50,000 from her husband's life insurance policy. After paying her several visits to learn what it takes to run a sloughing shed and soft-crab business, they are intrigued by Bonnie's offer to split the business three ways, with her acting as a manager and consultant since she has to care for her children. Two weeks later the twins move into her home; a move that over time will fulfill all their sexual needs, too.

It's not out of the realm of possibility that Bonnie would share her bed with a man or even twins so soon after the death of Vera's husband, Bud who fathered her first son, and Pretty Boy who fathered her younger boy before she married him two years ago.

Every evening, before climbing into bed between the twins, Bonnie removes all her clothes, preferring to sleep in the buff. Roland is always on her right side and Cary on her left, watching her methodically remove her undergarments and hang them neatly on hangers in the closet. Usually at this point, one asks the other, "Is it your turn tonight or mine?"

"Who's keeping score," the other one answers. "Isn't it nice that we don't have to chase a girl with big boobs anymore? All we have to do is nudge Bonnie and ask, "Are you ready for some *yum-yum*?"

The other one answers, "Now we know what is meant by 'watching out for the farmer's daughter.' They never seem to get tired or say, 'Not tonight. I have a splitting headache.'"

The following week, Abigail is given a surprise retirement party inside the R&D Lab at Ridgefield and presented with a painting of a Balinese dancer, painted by Antonio Blanco. "Whenever you look at it," says Kim, "remember, the dynamic way she's moving her body is the same way you kept things moving at Ridgefield."

"The brushstroke reminds me of the Italian impressionist Giovanni Boldini," says Sergio.

"I love it," says Abigail without hesitation. "What can you tell me about it?"

"We pitched in to buy it from Szymanski Gallery in Rock Hall," says Liz. "The owner gave us a discount after we explained the reason we were buying it. He said the artist was born in 1927 in Manila, studied in New York and settled in Campuan, Indonesia in 1955."

"Java Temple Dancer, c.1958" painted by Antonio Blanco (Born 1927 in Manila, Philippines).

"I've never seen an artist capture a woman's body gyrating as much as Blanco did with this Java dancer," says Sandy. "I wish I could capture the movement, but I'm better when working as a sculptor, using *pasteline*, a moist, non-hardening clay mixed with oil or wax. When the clay mold is cast in bronze, you can touch it, even hold it and feel a heart beating inside."

On a cloudy Wednesday two days after Labor Day Mark takes his early morning jog around Cylburn with Jen at his side. It's been two years but Jen is still getting acquainted and adjusted to the layout. She is especially confused when she sees her face and paws reflected in the still water of the Olympic-size swimming pool behind the mansion.

An hour later Mark is having a second cup of coffee and reading *The Sun* in his office when Jen pokes her head between his knees, pushing the papers out of his hands. "Whoa, Bessie, ah Jen. What's happened to you, girl?" he exclaims. "You're soaking wet. Did you get caught in the automatic sprinklers?"

Jen looks up at him with those eyes that stir his heartstrings and shakes her head from side to side. Mark dries her with a bath towel and gives her a massage to relieve her anxiety, then follows her wet tracks out of the mansion, which lead to the swimming pool. It doesn't take long for him to surmise that she must have fallen into the water. "Thank God she was determined to find a way out and eventually used the steps at the shallow end," he says, bending down to press his forehead against hers.

At 7:30 a.m. Mark hears the phone ringing when Lola calls through a window in the kitchen, "It's for you. I'll switch the call to your office."

"We wanted to catch you at home so as not to interfere with your work at the mill," says Abigail.

"It's about time we brought you up to date on what's going on at Swan Haven Marina since you bought out Jeanie Wayne," says Womble, joining in the conference call. "Glen Glenn has been a jack-of-all-trades after being interviewed in April and is working with Rachel Able Wayne, who remains the manager. Glen's wife, who has a degree in accounting from the University of Baltimore, is answering the phone, filing paperwork and running errands so Rachel can concentrate on what she does best, and that's sales."

"The consensus around here," says Abigail, "is that Rachel Wayne has kept everything running in good order since her husband Bud died last year and agreed to her settlement from his estate."

"As you may recall, she had a pre-nuptial agreement with her husband before they were married," says Abigail. "I suggested that we keep her on as manager."

"The scuttlebutt is that she's especially good when it comes to talking boat owners into long-term leases," says Womble.

"It appears that she's turning a decent profit for Ridgefield with a minimum of oversight from us," says Abigail.

"Rachel's never called me for any problems. As someone told me a long time ago, if it's not broken, let it alone," says Womble.

"Don't take anything for granted," says Mark. "No one is immune from embezzlers. I heard that one of the most trusted employees of Bayside Market had embezzled over $150,000 before he was caught and they didn't have insurance to cover the loss. No one knows what someone will do when money is sitting there in a bank account. It's like a piece of cheese, very tempting to a rat."

"We have an Operating Procedure Safeguard (OPS) setup so that any checks written for expenses over $1,000 require my or Womble's signature," says Abigail.

"Also, the Glenn family is living in the apartment over the marina office and enjoying their jobs," says Womble. "Even their son Junior, pitches in whenever he can fit it into his schoolwork, which comes first. He has just started his freshman year at Kent High in Worton."

"The Glenn family is too good to be true," Abigail tells Mark. "They're all trustworthy and hard-working."

"And Glen gives you credit for giving him a second chance after the pickpocket incident inside Lexington Market," says Womble.

After their conference call is concluded, Womble turns to Abigail and asks, "What do you know about the embezzler at Bayside Market?"

"Only from what I read in the *Kent News*," says Abigail. "I better speak directly to Jeff Carroll, owner of the market, and find out what happened there."

Within a few days both Abigail and Womble learned that one of Bayside Market's trusted employees, who had been with them for over five years, was writing checks to himself instead of making them payable to companies for bills outstanding.

"Since he was also doing the accounting," Abigail mentions to Mark on a subsequent conference call, "he could hide everything from Jeff until those companies complained about not being paid."

"By the time the shit hit the fan," says Womble, joining the conversation on the speaker phone in Abigail's office, "the bastard was hiding in South Carolina. It took detectives to find and arrest him and court filings to extradite him back to Maryland for trial. You can imagine the worry and misery it caused Jeff and his family."

Two weeks later, they are again on a third conference call to Mark. "I regret to tell you," says Abigail, "that, after hiring an accounting firm to go over the books at the marina, they found some serious discrepancies in 'accounts-payable.' It turns out that Rachel Wayne has been embezzling money in a scheme closely aligned to the embezzler of Bayside Market. She had customers write out their checks for leases 'payable to Rachel Wayne,' then cashed them and doctored the books so that it appeared that the leases were 'accounts receivable'."

"We only went back to the time you inherited the marina," says Womble. "It could be possible that she was pulling this fraud while married to Bud since she had complete control over the operation of the marina."

"We've turned the matter over to the district attorney for Kent County for prosecution because Rachel has disappeared from Rock Hall," says Abigail.

"How much money was embezzled so far?" asks Mark.

"Probably around $195,000 dollars for ten leases," Abigail says slowly and apologetically. "It's a shocking and revolting development since we held her in such high esteem and credited her for keeping the marina solvent. I was the one who convinced you to keep her on since it meant a good transition of the operation."

"My advice is to trace the money and find out where she spent it," says Mark. "The district attorney can get access to credit-card records and bank accounts. There are probably laws that prohibit us from putting a lien on her house, but we may be able to recover some money on whatever and wherever she spent our funds. In the meantime, it's a financial blow and an embarrassment to Ridgefield and our reputation for hiring good people. It could have been a lot worse. It's a lesson, perhaps a wake-up call, that we can all learn something from. There I go again ending a sentence with a preposition. Of course, Winston Churchill easily solved the problem by invoking the preposition rule: 'One rule up with which I will not put.'"

A week later, Abigail and Womble are on a conference call with the DA who tells them that Detective Mike McGrath checked Rachel's phone records and traced a number of calls to New Freedom, Pennsylvania and her credit-card expenses for gas at a petrol station there. He drove to the address associated with the Pennsylvania telephone number and found Rachel Wayne on a farm just over the border of Maryland in Pennsylvania."

"What did she have to say for herself?" Abigail asks.

"She was shocked. After talking things over with her boyfriend, she waived her right to fight extradition and will return to Maryland voluntarily."

"Did she have any of the money she stole from us?" asks Womble.

"No and yes," the DA answers quickly. "She didn't have more than a few hundred dollars in cash on her, but will plead guilty to fraud. She's agreed to turn over the deed to her farm, for which she paid $150,000, sell her house in Rock Hall and sign a promissory note that, if and when the house is sold, the balance due to Ridgefield will be deducted from the proceeds of the sale during escrow."

"I assume she's doing this in exchange for a lighter sentence from the judge and not because she's a benevolent soul, beholden to us," says Abigail.

"She said that she wants to come clean," says the DA, "and won't need the farm in New Freedom or the two bedrooms and two baths in Rock Hall. She told the detective, 'I'll be *downsizing,* at least for the next seven years behind bars,' which is the plea bargain I've recommended to the judge."

"That's good news, but what kind of farm did she buy in Pennsylvania?" asks Womble.

"A farm where you can eat as much meat, grain and soybean as you like every day, sleep as long as you want to, and have all the sex to keep you contented," says the DA, facetiously.

"Give me the address," Womble says. "On the other hand, there must be a catch somewhere. What's the catch?"

"You are confined to live in a two-foot by seven-foot stall or pen," says the DA. "It's not a farm for human beings. It's for hogs that produce the finest, tastiest and juiciest hams in the world, according to Rachel and her boyfriend. He's the reason she went there in the first place and bought his father's farm."

"How in the hell did she take up with a farmer from New Freedom?" asks Womble.

"Believe it or not, he was a correctional officer named Waverly Meadows who worked at the reception desk of FCI Cumberland when Rachel visited the federal correctional institution to see her ailing husband," says the DA. "It's easy to see why they were a good match. He was an officer who upheld the law and bared no liability to the fraud. She gave the order to buy the farm and told Detective McGrath that there was no need to make things harder for Waverly. She explicitly said she was not referring to his pecker."

"I fail to see the humor here," says Womble.

"Sorry about that," says the DA. "Apparently Waverly's father was about to lose the farm when processing plants were cutting back on their orders. Rachel stepped forward with the *doe-re-me* to fill his needs. I'm certain you can figure out what his needs were, other than financial."

"That's a *wham* of a story and Mark will never believe me when we tell him about it," says Womble, thanking him for his update.

"The plea bargain will save everyone, especially the state, a lot of money and misery," says Abigail, ending the conference call and falling back somewhat exhausted in her swivel chair. "However, it's imperative to exercise 'due diligence' after an asset is handed over to an employee who can swindle us with double-bookkeeping. From now on, we'll have an outside accounting firm go over the books at the marina bimonthly."

Chapter 7

On Wednesday around 4:00 p.m., after three weeks of classes at Kent High, Junior boards the bus for his return ride to Rock Hall. Thirty minutes later, he steps out of the bus, holding his knapsack of books in one hand and waving goodbye to the driver with the other. As he walks toward the marina office, he begins to limp and hides his face from his father, who needs his help to move a heavy bench on the porch. Junior is ashamed when asked about the bruises on his face and tells his father that he accidentally slipped down a stairway at school. When Glen touches his arms and shoulders, Junior grimaces a little and tries to hide the pain. "I can take the bruises, but not being able to make friends is painful," he tells himself.

His father suspects bullying and puts his arm around his shoulder. "Let's go for a walk down to the end of the pier." During the next hour he tries to gain his son's confidence, hoping he might open up or at least begin to explain the bruises.

"You may have been beaten up but you haven't been beaten," Glen tells his son. "You don't have to pretend with me. I'm here to help if you need it. I've always been proud of you but one thing I learned the hard way is never to lie."

"I have to think everything over, Dad, at least for another day. Not to worry. I can take the bruises and don't mind the name-calling either."

"What names?"

"An invader and *chicken-necker*," he says. "Why don't you go back to *Balamer* where you came from?"

"*Chicken-necker*, I've heard that name for outsiders who weren't born here," Glen tells him. "Bullying usually starts with name-calling."

"I could take care of them one at a time. What should I do if there's more than one ganging up on me?"

"Retreat and wait for another time, a better time, if that's possible. I've been afraid and scared many times in my life and often lost hope of ever finding a way to fight off the fear. But a person must never lose hope and confidence to do what is best at that time. And you must never give up. If they want to fight dirty, you can do the same. Whatever you do, don't let them get inside your head. That's private property, for you only."

The following day it's drizzling after the bus drops Junior off around four in the afternoon at Swan Haven Marina. He pulls his baseball hat down to his eyebrows, completely covering his forehead. His father is waiting outside the door to the marina office and anxious to find out how his third day in school went.

When Junior is reluctant to face his father, Glen realizes that something is wrong again and finds some new bruises on his face. "Don't tell me that you fell down some stairs again," Glen says. "Come clean and tell me everything that's going on at school. This could be serious."

His son drops his head onto his chest and tears form in his eyes. "A couple guys ganged up on me when I went to the bathroom between classes. They kicked me in the stomach, saying, 'This is for your father who's a *chicken-necker* too, and has a job when our fathers are outta work for a year.' I tried to beat them away as best I could, but they were too much to handle."

"Two against one is fighting dirty. I can show you a thing or two about fighting back, but it won't solve the problem," says Glen, gripping his fists and grinding his teeth.

"I thought school was a place for learning and making new friends," says Junior. "All I want is to walk in the hallways and be comfortable. They block me in and don't give me a chance to talk to other students. I'm beginning to hate myself. I don't know who to turn to for help at school and am ashamed to talk to the teacher. On the long bus ride back from school, I felt different, not accepted. I don't *fit in*."

"Not accepted -- by bullies?" Glen asks. "They're not in a position to judge you. Give me a few minutes to think this thing over. In the meantime your mother has a nice dinner waiting for you."

"I'm not hungry, Dad."

"You will be after you taste her sour beef and dumplings. It's an old recipe handed down from her grandmother. It'll stick to your ribs."

Within the next hour Glen is on the phone with Mark at Cylburn. "I'll get right to the point," Glen tells him. "It's embarrassing to talk something like this over with you because everyone at Ridgefield has been so good to us, but small towns have people with big ears and bigger tongues. Things get exaggerated and rumors fly faster than flies around horseshit."

"I can feel something brewing. Get to the point, Glen."

"My son, Junior, is being bullied at the high school. It started with taunting and calling him a *chicken-necker*, but now it appears that two boys gave him a good whipping inside the men's room."

"I remember the name calling when I first became a partner in the antiques business with "Annette's Antiques" in Betterton," Mark tells him. "They called me a *chicken-necker*, too. But when name-calling leads to fist-fights involving children, you've got to put a stop to it immediately. I've read too many bad things about bullying and the damage it does to kids and their families. There's no place for it in our society."

The following day, Glen drives his son to school and waits for an hour to see the principal, who is not surprised and tells him of his suspicion that taunting was going on but could never catch anyone fighting or willing to come forth as witnesses. "It's entirely up to the discretion of the principal," he tells Glen, "as to what action to take against the two perpetrators. But first I intend to meet with all the teachers and make them aware that anyone shirking their responsibilities may be furloughed. Then I'll schedule a general assembly of students."

'I realize that some students resent my boy for transferring from Patterson High in southeast Baltimore to Kent High in Worton," Glen tells him. "Perhaps they're jealous that he was in the top ten percentile of his class. But life is too precious and school is too important to see it wasted by taunting and bullying."

"School time at Kent High will not be wasted and bullying will not be tolerated as long as I'm principal. Added security may be an option. I'll hire a security guard with orders to pose as a custodian sweeping up the corridors and stairwells, but have him pay close attention to your son. I promise you that Junior will not be touched again."

The next mid-afternoon at Kent High, the security guard catches two seniors pushing Junior into a corner of the bathroom. Both are quickly escorted to the office of the principal, who tells them, "You're both suspended from school for a week. Laws against the practice of bullying are still being debated in Annapolis. However, you could face a civil suit if the victim's father decides to hire an attorney and make you pay for his son's injuries. Furthermore, I'll have to file a report with the Department of Education. This behavior will not be tolerated."

The next time Womble stops by the marina to hand Glen his paycheck, he learns of the bullying incident and tells him that he should never be ashamed to call him or anyone at Ridgefield for help. "That's what Ridgefield is all about," he tells him, "reaching out and helping those who can't find a way to help themselves out of a hole. You handled everything perfectly, just like you're handling Swan Haven Marina for us. If everything continues on course, you'll find a bonus in your Christmas stocking. We're all proud of you."

A few weeks later, as Glen is working at the end pier, he pauses to gaze out at the Chesapeake Bay Bridge. Suddenly, a gusher of water, reminiscent of Old Faithful in Yellowstone National Park, erupts out of the Bay and continues to spout water over sixty-feet high until a spirit emerges and is suspended there. It's the Spirit of the Bay who calls out, "Moses? Where in the hell are you?"

"There's no Moses here and I haven't a clue where he is," says Glen. "Have you checked on Mount Olives?"

"*Ya* mean, Mount of Olives, don't you?"

"Whatever," says Glen. "*Ya* better get to the point. I'm way behind in my work today."

"*Den* I'll get to the point," says the Spirit. "*Ya* did the right thing with *reportin'* the bullying to the principal."

"How do you know about that?"

"*Notin'* escapes my ears and eyes, my boy. *Dat's* why they made me the Spirit of the Chesapeake Bay. Keep up the good work, especially in caring for your family. And tell your boy, 'If he gives his best effort in whatever he does in school, everyone will be satisfied with the results,'" the Spirit says then spins like a toy top, leaving only a swirling funnel of white mist to mark his disappearance into the bay.

Chapter 8

In the middle of December with Baltimore covered in a blanket of snow, Mark sits at a table in his library at Cylburn to discuss plans from two developers, Richard Rizer and Ah Fong. They are two eager entrepreneurs who are interested in converting a portion of Sparrows Point shoreline, owned by Bethlehem Steel, into a dock for a new line of cruise ships. The two guests each taste a sample of Sara's assortment of finger sandwiches, freshly prepared as an appetizer.

"I'm happy that you're not asking Bethlehem Steel to convert a line of wartime cruisers into luxury ships, although the challenge would be intriguing," says Mark to 50-year old Baltimore native, Richard Rizer. Rizer's known throughout the east coast as 'Travel King Richard' with the reputation of giving his customers the satisfaction of 'Living like a Prince and Paying like a Pauper.'

"I envision a one week luxurious excursion line from Baltimore to the Virgin Islands," says Rizer, "We intend to make it so enticing with duty-free purchases that passengers will come again and again and tell their friends all about it, too."

Smiling and sitting to the right of Rizer is his partner, Ah Fong, Taiwanese billionaire with connections to Shanghai's biggest builder of cruise ships. He's watching every gesture and taking the measure of Mark. "We'll need a deep-water dock at Sparrows Point with a depth of at least 300-feet, a frontage 2,000-feet long and 1,000 feet wide for a parking lot and roads in and out of the terminal," says Ah Fong, chewing on every syllable.

"I like what I hear so far," says Mark. "Proceed with your proposal."

"If we lease a portion of your parcel at Sparrows Point," says Ah Fong, "we're prepared to pay for all the infra-structure needed on land, such as roads in and out of the terminal, buildings, electric power, fire, rescue, safety, and utilities. You would be responsible for everything water-wise along your shoreline on the Patapsco River, such as getting permits, especially permission to dredge, from the United States Department of the Environment (USDE), Department of Engineers (DE), and Baltimore City and County departments."

"And suppose we were to sell instead of lease you a portion of the parcel?" asks Mark.

"If we can come to an agreement to buy a section of Sparrows Point from Bethlehem Steel, we would be responsible for all costs," says Ah Fong, "but that offer would be predicated on getting approvals for all work to develop the terminal."

"What appeals to us is the fact that some of the inner structure is already in place since you have a railway into your mill," Rizer says, "but could be modified for a light-rail system. Since our meeting today is purely exploratory in nature, I don't have all the costs involved at this time, but we're probably looking at something in the neighborhood of five hundred million dollars to develop the Sparrows Point site."

"That's a nice neighborhood," says Mark. "Maybe you or another developer such as John Paterakis, developer of Harbor East and owner of H & S Bakery, would be interested in building a hotel on the property for guests who want to arrive a day early or stay a day longer in Baltimore. Your project would certainly benefit the city and state, give hundreds of workers a good paying job for several years and increase the assessment on the property which translates into higher taxes for our politicians to spend on projects that lobbyists are pushing for their clients. If you can pull it off, it's a win-win solution for an economy drowning in a recession."

After shaking his hand and expressing his thanks to Mark for a good first meeting, Ah Fong says, "On the way to your library, I passed a door and noticed a bronze in your kitchenette. Would you mind if I had a closer look at it?"

"Be my guest, Sir, and take all the time you need," Mark says, smiling with pride.

After Ah Fong touches the hind quarters of the horse, Mark says, "That must be a popular spot because my wife and children enjoy touching it there, too."

After studying the foundry marking stamped on the base and measuring its height with a small tape measure that Mark hands him, Ah Fong says, "Whenever you're ready to sell it, I'm ready to buy it."

"I'll have to talk to my wife first, but what price did you have in mind?"

"Five hundred thousand dollars."

"Is that U.S. dollars or Hong Kong dollars?

"U.S."

Mark turns and finds Lola in the doorway, nodding her head as a sign of approval. "I think you just bought our Remington bronze. If you write me a check, I'll wrap and carry it to your car."

"That has to be a 'wam-bam, thank-you ma'am, slam-dunk of a sale," Rizer says slowly and emphatically. "Szowee!"

After Mark puts the bronze, wrapped in a wool blanket, into the trunk of Ah Fong's car, he thanks him again and asks, "If you have another moment, would you mind telling me how you arrived at the price so quickly?

"If you must know…"

"I must. I must," says Mark, belly-laughing.

"Two years ago I was bidding on a Remington bronze at Christies in New York, which went way over their estimate of $500,000 - $700,000. Today I bought one of the same quality and vintage and didn't have to pay the buyer's premium, around 25 percent of the hammer price."

"You got a good buy, Mr. Fong, and good bye, Mr. Fong. Come again and soon," says Mark. "Perhaps next time you will find something that *goes* with the Remington bronze. Do you remember what an old art dealer, Joseph Duveen, said to his wealthy clients, such as Henry Huntington, J. P. Morgan, William Randolph Hearst, Samuel Kress, Andrew Mellon, John D. Rockefeller and Henry Clay Frick?"

"I heard about those collectors, but can't recall what Duveen said to them," says Ah Fong. "Refresh my memory, please."

"He said: 'Now that you bought that piece, don't let it get lonely. When you return, I'll have something special to put next to it.'"

"In that case you better have something for me next week," says Ah Fong, laughing. "I wouldn't want Remington to be alone for more than a week or two."

"One further thought for you, Mr. Fong," says Mark. "You mentioned that finding the Remington bronze here at Cylburn was better than bidding for one at auction. I venture to say that in the years ahead, you will discover the immense pleasure of gazing at *The Broncho Buster* again and again, and in time, will grow to appreciate it for what it is, not for what it's worth."

After Mark returns to the kitchen, he finds Lola helping her mother-in-law to remove pecan muffins from their tins. He tells them, "Duveen was one of the best art dealers in his time due to his intuition, a good eye, skilled salesmanship and reliance on the opinion of experts in the field. I have the intuition and in time, hope to acquire Duveen's other assets. There's always room at the top for success."

"America has a great deal of art and China has a great deal of cash money," says Lola. "Buying good art has always been a way of buying upper-class status, and we should help the Chinese to buy their way into immortality."

"Getting back to Duveen," says Sara, "I remember reading about him when I visited the Walters Art Museum, which is around the corner from Lola's office at Mount Vernon Place."

"I hate to introduce an element of dismay here, but something smells fishy," says Lola. "Why would the expert declare a fair-market-value of $50,000 and you sell it for ten times that amount?"

"Could it be that I'm a shrewd art dealer?" asks Mark, facetiously.

"Lola has a good point there," says Sara, joining in the controversy. "You're good, but not *that* good."

"Could it be that someone accidentally left a zero off the specified value?" asks Lola, persisting. "It's not the first time I've heard of this happening."

"This is a perfect situation to apply the former military policy of 'don't ask, don't tell,'" says Mark, spoken as if he were still an officer on active duty in the Navy.

"What's past is prologue," says Lola, "or, as one of my teachers in German said, '*Vas ist letzt ist vergangen und vergessen*,' which means 'What is past is gone and forgotten.'"

"With your permission, I intend to put our profit to good use by investing in people," says Mark. "The notion of creating a 'Back-to-Work' program has been bouncing around in my head for months. I foresee a program for unemployed people who need: first, a psychologist to help them to change their mindset and behavior; secondly, counselors who can work one-on-one and discover skills that they never knew existed inside them; and thirdly, instructors to guide them through a retrofit process, much like retrofitting a steel mill to improve its efficiency."

"The unemployed worker must trust your people and believe that he can change his ways," says Sara. "Otherwise you're just whistling *Dixie*."

"There must be a way to get people who are willing to work *back to work*," Mark says at the top of his lungs. "The future of America is at stake here, too."

After two weeks of more meetings, Mark, Richard and Ah Fong are still going over the blueprints for dredging out a dock when a telephone call from Mike Bloomburg tells them about news of a lawsuit. "When the Department of the Environment ran tests of the soil offshore, chromium was discovered in the top layer of sediment that blankets the entire shoreline of Bethlehem Steel at Sparrows Point," Mike explains on a conference call. "It is a chemical element that is considered a toxic waste residue, produced from the manufacture of armament before and during World II."

The following day Mark learns that a lawsuit was filed in federal court by the Chesapeake Bay Foundation (CBF) and the Baltimore Harbor Waterkeeper (BHW), as co-plaintiffs, against the current and former owners of the Sparrows Point steel plant. The petition seeks a full investigation of illegally discharging hazardous waste into the Patapsco River and Bear Creek, and clean-up of all pollutants. The plaintiffs are concerned for the health of neighbors, the protection of those who live, swim and fish there, as well as business owners who depend on customers living in and visiting Dundalk, and are demanding the restoration of Bear Creek and the Patapsco River.

According to the CBF president, the steel mill has been depositing toxic chemicals into these waters for decades and he demands an immediate investigation of the risks to human health and a halt to further pollution.

Shortly thereafter, residents and business owners in the Dundalk area around Sparrows Point complain of contaminated drinking water, and of toxic liquids and stench seeping out of the ground. They file a similar lawsuit against the owners of the steel mill. It's a double blow to Mark, Richard and Ah Fong that leaves them reeling back on their toes.

When Mark confers with Mike Bloomburg and his law partner, Lola Albright Hopkins, who has recently become Mark's wife, at their law office in Mount Vernon, the contents of the lawsuit are scrutinized as if they were specimens under a microscope. "The plaintiffs, neighbors and business owners in the area, accuse Bethlehem Steel of generating, storing and disposing hazardous waste at Sparrows Point without a permit for decades," says Mike. "That's quite an alarming charge."

"Furthermore," says Lola, studying the affidavit, "they claim, the mill is continuing with their dastardly acts in violation of the federal Resource Conservation and Recovery Act and related state laws. They also declare the toxic wastes include chromium, lead, zinc, naphthalene and benzene."

"At one location," says Mike, "readings for the presence of benzene, a known carcinogen, were one hundred thousand times the government's Acceptable Contaminant Level for groundwater."

"They mentioned the discovery of an underground hydrocarbon plume at Coke Point," says Mark, "which is at the southern tip of the mill, next to Bear Creek. They claim that it is moving underground, but don't specify the origin, rate and direction at which it's moving. It could be originating from Coke Point or perhaps from another location and passing under Coke Point on its way into Bear Creek."

After a long pause to wipe the sweat from his brow, Mark continues, "My great-grandfather began producing iron and steel and building ships over 100 years ago on about 2,300 acres. I'd like to believe that he always operated within the laws and was respectful of the environment even though there was little in the way of environmental regulation at that time. Turning a profit at the expense of harming the environment would never be written on his tombstone."

"If I was your attorney, and I am," says Lola, forcing herself to smile, "I would fight this lawsuit with a three-pronged attack. First, obtain a permit to drill test holes to investigate whether or not your mill is polluting the water or land, especially from pollutants, such as coke. If it is, you must admit the findings and take immediate corrective action. The truth will come out eventually, so don't hide any evidence. Use it to convince the plaintiffs that you have started on the right path to the restoration of the water and land of Sparrows Point."

"Go on," says Mark. "You have my undivided attention."

"Mine, too," says Mike.

"Secondly," says Lola, "appoint a research specialist to get access to government contracts with Bethlehem Steel, especially those written before and during World War II; and look for evidence that the government knew of the risks of pollution, but demanded the armament be produced as cheaply as possible to reduce their costs in wartime. If a General said, 'time and cost are essential factors now and we'll worry about contamination and pollution later,' we have some ammunition with which to fight back the plaintiff's claims."

"This is getting interesting," says Mike. "Now I know another reason why I made you an equal partner in the firm."

"Thirdly," Lola concludes, "hire the best scientist to study a way to reprocess these contaminants. Perhaps Liz and Kim can come on board with their idea of a vacuum to suck up the pollutants and send them directly to a floating laboratory for separation and reprocessing. It would be something like restoration of spent fuel rods in a nuclear reactor. Being close to those two ladies has *schooled* me in science.

Before the meeting is closed, Mike brings his copy of the lawsuit to his nose and gives a facial expression as if someone sprayed it with cow manure. "Do you both realize that the path you're headed down could lead to disaster?"

"More bad things to come?" asks Mark.

"What could be worse than what we already talked about?" asks Lola.

"Let's go back to the beginning where the developers are considering whether to lease or buy a section of the mill for their cruise line," says Mike. "Even if you sell them a part of the 2,300 acres, the USDE will watch every move. As soon as the land and shoreline is disturbed is a better word, you will be culpable for cleaning up your portion of the remaining parcel. I would recommend that, before any decision is made, you follow Lola's second point and find some evidence that the government knew of the danger of contamination when they entered into a contract with Bethlehem Steel decades ago and gave their authorization to proceed with the production of armament. If that evidence can be presented to the court, the government must be liable for the plume under the parcel, which is probably from the marinating and decay of waste products deposited at Coke Point, and liable for the metals deposited offshore."

After the meeting is completed, Mark drives Lola home for dinner and makes a circle around the Washington Monument, one of the many historical treasures of Mount Vernon Place and only a few blocks from her law office. "Walking or driving around it is supposed to bring you good luck," he tells her. "That's what George told everyone before he chopped down the cherry tree to make room for this granite edifice honoring the first president of these United States of America." He ends his words with a sharp salute to the monument.

"In that case," says Lola, "perhaps it's time to tell you something special that's going to happen to us."

"I'm listening, darling."

"I think that I'm pregnant."

"When will you know for sure?"

"When Dr. Rolf calls me with the test results from the lab. If it is confirmed, the stork will arrive in July."

Mark pounds the horn of his car with three short bursts followed by one long one.

"You should know that a policeman could give you a ticket for blowing a horn without due cause," says Lola. "But I doubt he would ticket you under the circumstances."

"Even if he gave me a ticket, do you think the judge would find me guilty under the circumstances?" asks Mark. "It's a means of celebrating a special occasion."

"If you were to get a ticket, I know a good lawyer who could get the case dismissed," says Lola, laughing and cuddling closer to him.

"Marvelous!" says Mark, taking his right hand off the steering wheel and squeezing her hand. "I better keep one hand on the steering wheel and get us safely back to Cylburn for a real celebration."

After coming to a stop in the Cylburn driveway, Mark draws his wife to him and gives her a warm embrace and loving kiss. "I'm glad we took that sleigh ride around Betterton two years ago," he tells her.

"You mean when I told you that I was falling in love with you?"

"And I said I wasn't ready to settle down."

"But you gravitated away from Sandy and eventually married Ruth," Lola says, sighing contentedly. "But I never gave up hope."

"Things have a way of working out with God's help, don't you think?"

"More than a little," says Lola, responding to his kiss with a stronger one.

Later that night, Mark and Lola are putting Jaime and Baby Ruth to bed and covering them with their favorite blankets. "I don't know about you but my insides are wound up tighter than a clock, still trying to digest the news that you broke to me earlier tonight. I should have suspected something was up. I've never seen you glow so brightly."

"Might be a good time for you to catch up on some emails," says Lola. "I'll make us a cup of hot decaffeinated tea with honey to calm our nerves."

Mark strolls into his study downstairs and opens a small window to let in some fresh air. A slight gust of wind turns a page of his weekly journal on his desk and lands on the last week of February and Ash Wednesday. On the left side of the journal are small photos of the German community in Baltimore celebrating a festival called *Fastnacht* or *Fasching*. The caption reads: 'Food and costumes play an important part in the celebration. Cooks spend days to marinate sauerbraten with red cabbage; rehbraten (very low-fat deer) with Juniper berries and Thuringia-style dumplings; and Bavarian-style schweinebraten, covered with gravy made from the roasted-pork's natural juices blended with wine or beer, butter and sour cream, served with potato dumplings and sauerkraut. Every epicurean will be drooling as party-goers spend endless hours opening trunks to find an old costume, such as a dirndl for the women and lederhosen for the men; in most cases, some alteration is usually needed to fit a bulging waistline.'

"I can't go to sleep either," says Lola, putting a cup of tea on the left side of his monitor. "I've invited Annette, Richard, Liz and Reggie to spend the weekend with us. Want to guess why?"

Before Mark can answer, Sara, dressed in a soft pink velvet robe, walks into the study and squirms into a lounge chair, with her feet propped up on the ottoman. "I'm not sleep-walking, believe me," she tells Lola. "It's my nerves and my heart telling me that I'm going to be a grandmother again. I've never felt quite like this before, probably because you are special, someone who was with me when I lost Mark's father. Ruth gave me my first granddaughter, Baby Ruth, but you always gave me hope for a better life ahead."

"Welcome to our little midnight klatch," says Lola. "Now, Mark, I asked you to guess why I invited Annette, Richard, Liz and Reggie to spend the weekend with us."

He puts his hand to his forehead, imitating a mind-reader, and says, "My intuition tells me it has something to do with Ash Wednesday and *Fastnacht*. I can't wait to see them again and hear what they're up to nowadays."

"I've made a reservation for Friday night at the *Rathskeller* in the basement of the Fifth Regiment Armory, where people of German descent celebrate with good food and dancing. I often went there during my studies at the University of Baltimore."

"*Ausgezeichnet, mein schatz*," says Mark, imitating his German professor at Hopkins and laughing at his accent. "I went there a few times when I was studying at Hopkins. I'll never forget the taste of their homemade sauerbraten with dumplings and draft beer from barrels imported from Munich."

"Speaking of German food, I'd like to make sour beef and dumplings for everyone next Sunday," says Sara, smiling. "But I'll take a rain check on going to the armory. My dirndl won't fit me anymore anyway!"

Chapter 9

The following Friday around 7:00 PM, after their drive from Betterton to Baltimore, Reggie and Liz, and Richard and Annette settle down in their respective bedrooms on the second floor of Cylburn and admire some of the artwork Mark and Lola have acquired.

"I remember when Ruth bought the portrait of the beautiful lady in red at auction in Crumpton," says Annette. "How her eyes would follow you when you walked by her."

"You mean this one?" asks Richard, pointing to it hanging on a wall above a chest of drawers. "You're right as usual. The eyes do follow you. I just tried it out."

Inside an adjoining bedroom, Liz takes Reggie's arm and leads him over to a bronze pedestal on which is a bronze of a semi-nude with a robe that has dropped to her waist. "Does this remind you of anyone?" Liz asks, knowing full well the answer.

"I'll have to think about it a moment," Reggie answers, giving her a long kiss. "Ah, yes, now it comes to me. It took a kiss to light the bulb over my head."

"Well, I'm waiting," Liz says.

"It's you, darling, when you posed for Sandy," says Reggie. "I seem to remember seeing the clay model on exhibit at the museum in Hagerstown a few years ago, too."

An hour later, everyone has changed into their German costume; the women wear a colorful, low-cut traditional dirndl that shows off their bosom and shapely legs while the men wear green lederhosen with a red stripe down the sides.

After a round or two of toasts, including one for Lola, who tells them about her pregnancy and is conscious about drinking any alcohol, Mark drives his mother's Mercedes 500 sedan for a 15-minute trip downtown to the Fifth Regiment Armory on Howard Street, named after Col. John Eager Howard, the Revolutionary War patriot.

It doesn't take long before they are served six steins of specially-prepared draft beer imported from Munich. In between toasts the men lead their wives around the dance floor. It's next to impossible to carry on a conversation when the band is playing because the blare from brass instruments of an old fashioned beer-hall band echo off the concrete block walls and easily could drown out any words. But no one gives a damn because it's *Fastnacht*, a time of celebration, a time to lose your inhibitions for a few hours. When the band takes a fifteen-minute break between sets of music, it's time to toast each other with memories of their days spent on the Eastern Shore. After several hours, the band master thanks everyone for coming and tells the crowd that it's time to place their last order of beverages. Reggie and Liz offer to buy everyone a nightcap.

A husky waitress, with muscles bulging under the sleeves of her dirndl, sets three steins of beer in each hand on their table. At that precise moment two husky men leave their table in the back of the armory, walk casually past Mark's table and nod as if they knew him.

After climbing the marble steps out of the armory, they stroll leisurely down Howard Street where their car is parked in the middle of the block. Before the driver turns the ignition key to start the motor, they synchronize their watches to read 11:30 PM then gaze up to admire the full moon shinning down and reflecting off the dashboard. They drive slowly through downtown Baltimore, passing several block parties in German neighborhoods as hundreds are still celebrating *Fastnacht*.

Thirty minutes later they walk up to the entrance of Bethlehem Steel and, after reaching the main gate, sneeze twice; they cover their mouth and nose quickly with a handkerchief then flash their ID badges and give the password to the security guard on duty. "Better take care of that cold before it develops into pneumonia," says the guard, noticing the white mist coming from their mouths and turning around to read the temperature on a thermometer hanging on the chain-link fence. It reads: 35 degrees Fahrenheit. He is agitated by an unexpected cold breeze coming across the Patapsco River and pays little attention to their identity cards, quickly waving them into the steel mill. "They're on time for the midnight swing shift," he says to himself. "My fuckin' watch has stopped running. Either the battery is dead or I'm dead from standing on my feet for two hours in this freezing cold fuckin' wind."

A minute later the two men overpower a security guard standing outside the ground-floor door to the control room of the cold-rolling steel production line. After tying and gaging him, they drag him into a nearby storage closet.

After checking the time again on their watch, they rush into the control room. Seconds later, they are holding revolvers at the head of the computer controller Giuseppe Guardi, who can trace his ancestry all the way back to his great great great great grandfather, Francesco Guardi, the renowned 18th century Venetian painter. They threaten to kill him unless he throws the manual override lever on the control panel to shut down the production line, which is not the correct action for a safe shutdown.

Fearing for his life, Giuseppe pleads with an Italian accent and shivering hands, "You *soms* of bitches! This is madness. Do *you* know what you're asking me to do? We could all be blown to smithereens by the explosion."

The taller of the two thugs gives him a blow to his chin which knocks him backward into the arms of the other thug. Shaking all over and barely able to stand on his feet, Giuseppe lowers his head and says a quick prayer.

"Come on, man. Do you want a bullet instead of another fist?" asks the shorter one. "Prayers won't be of much help. If you want to stay alive, do what we told you to do and do it now."

Giuseppe gazes at the console but can't bring himself to pull the lever then collapses on the floor. The shorter thug, watching carefully Giuseppe's eyes when they were telling him to throw the manual override lever, sees a longer handle -- called a gang -- that allows the controller to throw a row of five switches all at once. He pulls on the gang and immediately white, yellow and orange-colored sparks ignite explosions throughout the plant.

Five robots that control the crucibles of molten steel go berserk, slowly turning in random directions and eventually pouring out their contents. When the 1,600 degrees-Centigrade liquid steel hits the ground, it splatters, sending sparks and particles of steel in all directions. The explosions quickly transform the factory into an inferno. Unexpected bursts of intense white light cast shadows that look bizarre and resemble images from a Rorschach test. Intermittent popping sounds from short-circuited thermocouples, attached to the crucibles to measure the temperature of the liquid steel, echo off the concrete block walls of the mill.

From a distance it seems that the molten metal oozes into all pathways of the production line, but actually it moves quickly, hotter than a blowtorch. A fiery thunderstorm spreads randomly and resembles hot lava flowing down the side of an erupting volcano. Hardly anything is recognizable because of the flames, fumes and steam produced when hot metal makes contact with the cold concrete pad. What was once an efficient production line begins to turn into ruins, burning like the city of Rome while Nero fiddled. Alarms go off everywhere inside the mill, as well as one sent automatically to the Sparrows Point Firehouse. Fifteen minutes later three fire companies arrive with their sirens blaring in the frigid night air.

Two neighbors, living in the middle of a row house across from the mill, poke their heads out a second floor window; one of them says, "They better not be wasting tax-payers money to celebrate *Fastnacht*." The other responds, "That's no celebration. It looks like a bombardment of cannons firing across the Patapsco and landing on Sparrows Point."

Soon fire fighters, wearing Hazmat gear, race through the plant, make an assessment of the fire and search for night-shift personnel. They quickly discover the security guard inside a storage bin next to the control center. He tells them to check inside the control room. A minute later, two fire fighters carry Giuseppe Guardi out of the plant on a stretcher; he is semi-conscious and in pain.

As fire fighters check the mill for toxic fumes and make a second search for personnel who may have been injured, Fire Chief Don Orsini checks his watch and notes the time: 1:00 AM. "This is the moment I hate in this job, having to wake someone up and tell them their home has burned to the ground," he says to himself. After turning around to give more orders to his fire fighters, he walks out of the mill and telephones Mark at his home.

"We've met before," he tells him, "so I'll get right to the point. There was an explosion inside your mill. One of your workers told me it's the furnaces near the cold-rolling steel production line."

Before the Fire Chief can continue, Mark interrupts him by asking, "Are there any casualties?"

"Two, so far. One of them, a security guard, was found bound and gagged inside a storage room. He's OK and refused to go to the hospital. However, a tech named Giuseppe Guardi was found inside the control room. He is semi-conscious and inside an ambulance on its way to Sinai Hospital. Three other workers made it safely out of the plant. No one needed treatment in a hyperbaric chamber for smoke inhalation. Other than those two, we found no casualties at this time. But our search is far from over. We expected to find more workers, but thank God, they may have been on a work-break or were getting ready for a shift-change."

"What can I do, Chief?" asks Mark.

"One thing you cannot do is come to the plant right now. Your production line is a mess. We used several thousand gallons of water, along with hundreds of gallons of foam concentrate to quell the inferno. Your plant is still smoldering, with sporadic smoke along with toxic fumes coming from hydraulic oil. Obviously, the plant will need monitoring and be quarantined until further notice."

"Thanks, Chief," Mark tells him. "Keep me advised and if anyone wants to know where to contact me, you can tell them that I'm heading to Sinai to check on Giuseppe Guardi."

After repeating the news about the explosion at the mill, he tells his wife, "I've got to get to Sinai as soon as possible to check on one of my men."

"Whatever you do, drive carefully," says his wife. "He's in good hands at Sinai."

As Mark leaves his bedroom, he finds York and Reggie dressed in fleece-lined parkas and heavy overcoats over their pajamas. "We're going with you to the hospital and don't try to stop us," says Reggie. "York will drive his car and you can think about making any phone calls to your staff. Get ready to give orders, even to us."

During the 20-minute drive to Sinai Hospital, Mark calls his Chief Engineer, Joost de Wal, at his home and, after explaining the situation, tells him, "Stay home until you hear from me. The mill is quarantined. Get hold of someone in personnel and call all the workers in that section of the mill to stay home but be on call until further notice. You can also tell them they will still be paid and won't lose any benefits. A supervisor may want to switch them to another section of the mill."

A half-hour later, Mark is pacing the corridor on the second floor and waiting for the doctor or nurse to come out of Giuseppe's recovery room. He finishes saying a prayer as Dr. Joe McLain, the attending physician, gives his permission and says, "He's sleeping, but at least you can go in to have a look, if that's what you want to do."

Mark is relieved to see his controller alive, but with his skull bandaged. It's hard for Mark to resist touching his head. The sound coming from one of the heart monitors is a quiet steady staccato of beeps. Mark looks at the monitor and sees no erratic spikes. He remembers being hooked up to similar monitors four years ago when he was implicated in Vera's murder.

Around 9:00 AM Mark gets a phone call at his home. It's Dr. McLain on the line, giving him some good news about Giuseppe. "He's awake and sitting up in bed," says Dr. McLain, "and angry that he missed Sunday church services. More importantly, he refuses to eat anything until he can talk to you. So arrange to get here as soon as you can, please."

Thirty minutes later, Mark is standing beside Giuseppe's bed on the second floor of the Chester River Hospital in Chestertown. "It looks as if you're still watching electronic monitors," he tells him. "You don't need anyone's permission to forget those monitors and have a good look at the pretty nurses around here. But you'll have to do it before your wife comes to see you later. If she catches you pinching one of the nurses, like they do in Rome, you better be prepared for a wallop."

Giuseppe smiles then grimaces as he tries to slid down in his bed and pull the sheets over his head. He doesn't have the strength because of the sedatives given by Dr. McLain. "I feel like I'm sleeping on a cloud, *padrone*."

"Rest easy, my friend. Mother always told me it's the best way to sleep."

"Everything happened so fast. One moment I'm working at the console and when I turn around, two thugs are holding Magnums at my head like in a *Dirty Harry* movie. Then the taller one *cold-cocked* me in my jaw. I think it was his fist. He might have had brass-knuckles."

"One thing at a time, *paisano*. Let's get you back on your feet, then you can tell us what happened at the mill."

"I can't wait, boss. All I remember is them giving me the orders to shut down the plant. Everything is still *kinda* fuzzy."

"You did the right thing," says Mark. "Thank God you're alive. In the military we honor a good soldier like you by pinning a medal to his chest. In your case I'll pin a SEAL trident to your skullcap."

"If it kept you alive in Iraq, it's like a St. Christopher medal."

"When our personnel carrier was struck by a grenade missile, I was the only one who made it back alive. It means a lot to me, but so do you."

After leaving his room, Mark finds Dr. McLain standing in the corridor, reviewing some phone messages handed to him by a nurse. "On the surface," Dr. McLain tells him, "Giuseppe may seem normal to you, but he has all the symptoms of Post-Traumatic Stress Disorder (PTSD). He believes that he contributed to the explosion by not sacrificing his life, or doing something to save the mill."

"I know the feelings, Doc," says Mark. "I served in Iraq. Years after one of the SEALS in my squad died I still feel guilty that I didn't do more to save his life."

"My recommendation is for him to take a month off," Dr. McLain continues, "and get completely away from the mill; perhaps spend this spring near the Chesapeake Bay where he and his family can enjoy the peace and quiet of nature and God's graces."

"Whatever you believe is best for Giuseppe is best for us. He's more than a devoted worker. He's part of our family and I intend to see that he gets the best of care."

Around 8:00 PM, after the Fire Chief tells him that it's safe for him to enter the plant, Mark is anxious to have a look around at the mess. Thirty minutes later, his chief engineer, Joost de Wal, wearing a Netherlands Olympic Team ski suit to protect him from the frigid temperatures outside, walks into Mark's office. He notices him applying a bag of ice cubes to his right ankle and says, "Don't tell me you broke through the barricade like in your days as a SEAL. You told me the plant was quarantined. What's going on with your ankle?"

"I wasn't paying attention and slipped on some hydraulic oil that must have spattered on the fire fighters," says Mark. "I just twisted my ankle. It's nothing to worry about. This icepack will keep the swelling down."

"Are you in any pain?" asks Joost. "Should I get you a crutch or cane?"

"Not unless I broke something or tore a ligament. The pain is nothing compared to the migraine that came on after seeing the devastation here."

After pausing to watch Mark tie the ice pack around his ankle, Joost says, "I hate to be the one to add more misery to this catastrophe, but the 'super' is missing. His name is Captain William Richard Jones. Everyone called him 'WR'. He's been with the mill for 15 years; a superintendent for two years. He was well-respected by his men and had many friends here. A fireman found one of his shoes with the laces untied. It appears that he may have been trying to disable a robot or uncouple a ladle. We suspect that he accidentally slipped and fell into a crevice filled with molten steel."

"God have mercy on his soul," says Mark, swiveling his chair around so that it faces the wall behind his desk. He bows his head, covers his face with his hands and cries uncontrollably for the next thirty seconds. When he regains his composure, he rises from his desk, walks over to a corner of his office and looks at a small cross then says a silent prayer.

"I don't remember meeting him," he tells Joost. "Was he the old timer who forgot to zip up his fly?"

"He was a good man," says Joost, dismissing Mark's question, "who loved the mill more than anyone I ever knew here. Everyone knew what he meant when he would say, 'we'll get this job done on schedule, no matter how long it takes!' We kidded him about forgetting to zip up his pants after going to the john. I'm not trying to be funny; I just want you to know , he was a character right out of Damon Runyon, with steel in his blood. I don't think he ever took a day off for sick leave." When he fails to get a response from Mark, he asks him, "Are you with me?"

"I hear you loud and clear," says Mark, heart-broken. "I was thinking about Thomas Paine who said 'These are the times that try men's souls. The first thing I learned in the military was that an officer takes care of his men. Make an investigation, review all safety procedures and do whatever you can to safeguard the loss of life or injury and prevent or minimize this tragedy from ever happening again."

"We'll get through this nightmare," says Joost, "and everyone will learn something and be stronger from it. Adversity brings out the best in good people. Thank God the damage was what it was. It could have been a lot worse."

Four days later, at the funeral service for WR, five of his co-workers leave their pews to speak from the pulpit. The first told about WR's desire to hire men who were young and ambitious; the second mentioned his way of creating a strong but pleasant rivalry between different sections of the mill; the third pointed out his way of hiring men of mixed nationalities and races; the fourth touched on his insistence on keeping each shift at eight hours, stating 'physical and mental strength cannot stand the ordeal of unwarranted overtime;' finally, the fifth cited his quest to pay attention to those working nearby in case you have to take over their job in an emergency.

At the last minute, Joost de Wal motions to the priest that he would like to offer a few words apropos to the occasion. After taking a position near the front pew, he says, "Some of you have heard the expression 'He's sleeping on the job.' Well, WR occasionally did just that but not in the way you may be thinking. When a problem popped up, he'd find a quiet corner in which to catch his breath and pause for a few winks, long enough to recharge his batteries. Afterwards, he always managed to come up with a solution, one that only he could devise. As I've told him many times, 'You are more than a supervisor. Steel is in your blood.'"

After pausing to look at the faces of everyone in attendance, Joost continues, "Bethlehem Steel was very fortunate to have him as one of the leaders of our team. He will be greatly missed."

As everyone makes their way out of the church the skirl of a bagpipe is heard.

Chapter 10

Over the next two weeks, Mark and his staff are busy trying to assess the damage and find the perpetrators who sabotaged the plant. Because the production line was in the middle of filling a government contract, the FBI is called in to head up the investigation with the support of the Baltimore City Police Department. The combined effort is called a Joint Terrorist Task Force (JTTF), under the supervision of Buster Browne.

Three days later FBI agent, Charlie Magnante gets his wish to transfer from a desk job at the bureau in Washington and join the JTTF team of five investigators to perform an entire physical surveillance of the cold-rolling mill. On his first day on the job, he gets a phone call from Mike Bloomburg. "Tell Buster that I've had trouble contacting him and request that he approve my adding a special investigator by the name of Virgil Tubbs, who would be a liaison between JTTF and Bethlehem Steel," Mike tells him. "He would be an asset and work under his supervision. We've had great success with him on the job a few years ago when he solved the murder of the mother of Mark's young boy, Jaime."

Two days later Virgil discovers an iPhone being charged in a receptacle inside the corner of a bottom shelf along the hallway leading to the computer room. Using protective gloves he disconnects it, places it in an evidence bag and hands it to Charlie Magnante, who marks it for analysis by the FBI forensics lab.

By the middle of April, Buster and his team are still operating from an office in another part of the mill and scrutinizing copies of fingerprints found on the phone, along with a transcript of the telephone numbers and digital recordings. During more than a month of intensive investigation, the fingerprints on the phone are confirmed as those of two inspectors who had access to the mill. Bethlehem Steel was forced to hire them in accordance with the bargaining agreement between the company and the steel-workers union. When photographs of the two men are shown to Giuseppe Guardi, he confirms that they were the same men who ordered him to shut down the plant.

"We've had a major breakthrough in the case," JTTF Chief, Buster Browne, tells Mark, Lola and Mike on a conference call. "Along with the positive identification by Guardi of the two men who took over the control room at BS, the telephone numbers on the cell being charged at the mill were traced to Lester 'Les' Rook, a multimillionaire. He was a well-connected bigwig in political affairs due to his millions made during the dot-com boom. By the way, he was also the father of Captain Ira Rook. Do any of these names ring a bell with you?"

"Loud and clear," says Mark, "but continue with your news."

"We've discovered that these two thugs were seen roving in areas of the plant that had nothing to do with inspecting workers on the cold-rolling production section. Several workers told us that they spotted them walking off distances around the control room, as if they were making a time and motion study; this behavior had nothing to do with their responsibilities for which they were hired."

"Who would have thought they would turn against their fellow workers?" says Mark. "Each was a Judas."

"Based on the physical evidence inside the phone," Buster continues, "I suspect that the two men were acting under the pretense of being inspectors in the plant and knew enough about the layout to quickly gain entry before an alarm could be thrown."

"Instead of tabulating the number of man hours to complete a production run," says Mike Bloomburg, "they were most likely hired by Les Rook to wreak havoc and destroy the mill in retaliation and vengeance against Mark for being the catalyst in the court martial of his son, Captain Ira Rook."

"We'll need more time to find out if the union played a part in the sabotage," says Buster.

"I can't wait to get my hands on Rook, says Mark. "When you corner that rat, don't do anything until I can get my hands on him first."

"Revenge is sweet but justice is better," says Buster. "Furthermore, you'll have to wait your turn to get at Rook. We want to take him alive if we can."

The following day, while a warrant is being arranged for the arrest of Rook, Buster probes deeper into the lives of the two thugs. He learns that they were on the personal staff of R. L. Stackhouse, former union president before Franz Beckenbauer took over control. "When they were assigned to work at the mill," says Buster to Mark and Mike on a conference call, "Franz had nothing to do with that decision; it was left up to the personnel director of the union to make all assignments."

Twenty-four hours later, both saboteurs are behind bars after warrants for their arrest are served. During subsequent interviews, their public defender has convinced them to make a plea bargain with the DA. In exchange for a plea of guilty, they will turn state's witness and testify that Les Rook was the mastermind behind the plot to destroy the mill. "He planned every step of the operation," says one, "including giving each of us a cell phone so that we could call him any time of the day."

"That cell phone proved to be the 'smoking gun' when the voices on the recordings matched those of Les and his two hired thugs," says Buster to Mark during a late hour telephone call to Cylburn. "The technology used by our agents is the result of research and development by personnel of IBM. I can't thank them enough for making our job to serve the American people better and better. I take my hat off to them."

"Was it a smartphone?" asks Mark.

"That would depend on how smart people are who use it," says Buster, laughing. "Actually, it was an iPhone; amazing that those two *bug wits* now behind bars knew how to use it."

"Don't be amazed, Chief," says Mark. "My five year old son, Jaime, knows how to open a cell and dial 911 or me at the office."

The next morning Buster is briefing his top aide, C. Alvin Kissinger, whose uncle worked in the State Department thirty years ago. "It appears," says Buster, "that Les Rook was a great manipulator who always managed to be one step ahead of everyone. He even got inside information from the FBI and local police agencies. He must have had many sleepless nights over how to take revenge after Mark discovered a canister of mustard gas that led to his son's court martial."

"But now Les is cornered and he must know that it is only a matter of time before JTTF comes knocking on his door with an arrest warrant," says C. Alvin, speaking like his uncle in a bass monotone.

On the last Friday of April, around 8 pm, after having dinner served to him in the grand dining hall of his mansion, tucked away in a remote hill of Hunt Valley, Les Rook's butler asks with a distinctive British accent, "You didn't touch your apple strudel, Master. Was it not to your liking?"

"If anyone should ask you if I touched my dessert, you can answer truthfully that I did," Les tells him, putting both index fingers into the strudel.

"That is a strange reaction from him," the butler says to himself. "Maybe it has something to do with the winds and storm clouds forming outside. He's been acting mighty peculiar all day, bordering on the bizarre, such as asking the cook to make a guacamole dip. He's never eaten avocadoes before."

Thirty minutes later, Les dismisses his staff, wishes them a good weekend and takes a stroll with his female German shepherd dog around the grounds behind the mansion. He throws a large bone in the direction of a huge pine resting on a knoll, from which the estate gets its name, and admires how fast she retrieves it. After filling his lungs with the cool evening air, he admires his thoroughbreds that enjoy their peaceful teasing one another in rich green pastures. He says with a sense of regret, "I should be down there, enjoying the good life instead of up here, facing the consequences of my vengeance."

Moments later he puts his Shepard in her kennel and walks into his garage. He pauses at the rear door to take a long look at his pristine 1955 Bentley with a burgundy sheen. An image flashes across his mind; a hose connected from the exhaust pipe into the car. "I'll take everything under advisement. No need to rush things. Everything in due time," he repeats several times before walking through a short corridor connecting the rear door of the garage to a side door of the mansion.

A minute later he opens the top drawer of the desk in his study and touches the barrel of a .357 Magnum revolver. At that moment a bolt of lightning strikes somewhere close to his property that causes a flicker of electricity, followed by an unexpected torrential rainfall. He moves some letters from the top of his desk over the gun and leaves the drawer open.

Moments later he looks at his watch that indicates 9 pm and opens the main electric panel at the rear of the house to switch 'off' all the breakers, except for one room. For the most part the mansion is completely covered in darkness, except for the bursts of lightning shining through stained-glass windows and reflecting off highly-polished hardwood flooring.

Two hours later all is quiet inside the mansion except for a cat, meowing at the end of the hallway. Outside, a barrage of thunder echoes around the farm, sending the horses galloping into their pole barn. One exceptionally loud thunderbolt makes some of the old latches on the stained-glass windows rattle and causes Les to shutter a little. Torrential rain follows the sounds of thunder.

Suddenly two patrol cars speed up the driveway of the mansion as their headlights shine on a weathered sign that reads: 'Lone Pine Farm.' Both drivers lean forward on the steering wheel to catch a good look at the sign between swipes of the windshield wipers. Other occupants see lightning striking near the stone wall with its parapets and buttresses; it gives the mansion the appearance of a medieval fort. "I wonder if we should be wearing a spark-arrester or ground-wire so we don't get electrocuted in this heavy rain," says C. Alvin, his top aide who sits uncomfortably in the back seat of the first car.

When the drivers jam on their brakes near the main entrance, both cars are speeding so fast they screech and slide to a halt, leaving a four-inch gulley in the crushed gravel of the driveway. Their headlights are left on to illuminate the front door area. "Strange that even the driveway lights are off," says Buster, sitting nervously in the passenger seat of the first car. "I hope everyone remembers to be ready for the unexpected. That means a revolver in one hand."

Jumping quickly out of the cars are JTTF personnel, each wearing a dark blue jacket with large yellow letters 'JTTF' on the backside and carrying a flashlight in one hand and a gun in the other. They scatter to a pre-determined position until the entire mansion is surrounded by agents. Buster unbuttons his jacket and removes a .347 Magnum from its holster, which is attached to a Kevlar protective vest. Then he pushes the doorbell and waits a few seconds. "I can't hear it ringing inside and don't see a light anywhere," he says to the agents standing behind him.

"Awesome knockers," says C. Alvin, noticing two antique cast-iron knockers on the front entry door.

"Oh, thank you, C. Alvin," says Gloria Floria, a six-foot, buxom 25-year old newcomer to the taskforce who arches her back and looks down at her firm bosoms. "I didn't think you noticed them under my flak jacket."

C. Alvin quickly turns his head towards Buster and says, "Use the knocker and slam it hard, Chief."

"Do you have any other brilliant suggestions, *Sherlock*?" say Buster, grimacing as he slams the antique knocker so hard that the entire doorframe rattles. "Is that what you had in mind? The dead buried in a cemetery must have heard that knock now reverberating in my ear drum."

"Those parapets were originally used to defend the building from military attacks, but now they prevent the spread of fires," says

C. Alvin, glancing upward at the crenellated roofline. "According to his butler, Rook dismissed everyone for the weekend after finishing his dinner. I wonder if he's still here or was tipped off that we were on our way."

Twenty seconds later, one of the agents uses a passkey to gain entry to the massive front door. Four agents move cautiously behind Buster and begin to scour the front premises with their flashlights to guide their way. "Find the main circuit breaker to get some lights on so we can see what we're doing," Buster shouts out.

A moment later a bolt of lightning reflects off a pair of large mirrors hanging in the middle of the hall just as Gloria steps through a doorway. She sees a silhouetted figure pointing a pistol at her and fires three shots at the image. One of the mirrors shatters into large pieces that crash to the ground with a sound that sends shivers up the spline of Woody Woods, an agent standing nearby. "No time to get trigger happy, kid," he says, wiping some sweat from his brow. "That was a close call."

"Better to fire first and be alive," says Gloria, taking a breather and looking down at her pistol. "It sometimes has a mind of its own and reacts instinctively in pressure situations. I'm glad you weren't hurt."

Daniel "Dandy" Dann, one of the older agents with the bureau for over 20 years, finds the main circuit breaker panel in the utility room. Holding his flashlight in his mouth, he turns off one by one each of the branch circuit breakers then resets the main breaker, causing lights to go on throughout the house. Another agent with a pigtail running under the back of his cap pokes his head through the doorway, gives him a high-five and tells him, "Nice work, Dandy. The house is lit up like a Christmas tree."

He closes the door of the panel box, taps it gently and says, "Good boy," then turns to the agent and says, "It's a 300-amp panel. The breakers may have tripped from a lightning strike."

Another agent hollers from the library at the far end of the hall, "He's not in here," and takes a second look around to scan the book shelves to see if there may be a secret passage door out of the library.

"He's not here, either," says another agent, calling out from the drawing room then striking some keys on the baby grand. "A Steinway is always in tune."

"Not up here," says a third agent, coming out of a bedroom, who uses his flashlight to find the hand-rail then descends the stairway from the second-floor balcony.

A fourth agent, using a pass key to open a room opposite the library, hollers down the hall, "Chief, I think you better come here."

As Buster walks down the wide hall furnished with antique furniture, statues and paintings, he says to his men, "The owner will not be pleased to see the muddy footprints all over his house, but that's the least of his problems."

When Buster enters the far room, he first sees a dim light coming from a Tiffany lamp on a pedestal in one corner; there are six iridescent-gold glass lampshades, each shaped in the form of a lily. In the middle of the room is a heavy-set man sitting in his chair and slumped over a five-by-eight-foot platform, filled with a display of model trains, depots and colorful signs. Even artificial weeds are scattered throughout the display for added realism. Along the outermost track is a row of box cars hooked together; one is a-freight car, filled with a mush that looks like pale-green oatmeal. A continuous beep is heard from a blinking railroad crossing barricade that is malfunctioning and slowly moving up and down near the man's head. His left hand clutches a replica of a Baltimore and Ohio Railroad locomotive; the other is partially inside a bag of tortilla-chips.

"Don't touch anything until McDonald gets a 360-degree scan of the room with his *Panoscan* camera," Buster shouts loud enough for everyone to hear on the first floor of the mansion. Five minutes later, Buster removes a train conductor's hat and turns the man's head slightly to check his carotid artery for a heartbeat. "Nothing here either," he says facetiously, taking a cigarette out of his mouth. "If you're *gonna* die, is there a better way to go than playing with your toys?"

"The only difference between men and boys is the price of their toys," says C. Alvin. "He fits the description of Les Rook. In a dim light I'd swear he was Alfred Hitchcock."

"Who did you say?" says Buster.

"Hitchcock, the film director," says C. Alvin. "By the way, did you hear the story about one morning when he got on a digital scale in his bathroom, one with a computer-generated voice that calls out your weight?"

"You mean a scale designed for those who can't see over their big tummy like mine and read the dial?" asks Buster. "No, I didn't hear the story about Hitchcock and his bathroom scale. What's so strange about that?"

"When *Hitch* got on the scale," says C. Alvin, a voice said 'Please, only one at a time!'"

"I don't know what I'd do without your chatter," says Buster. "It always lightens the situation. Call the coroner. I can't wait to find out the cause of death."

"Do you mind if I pay my last respects to the *habeas corpus* or is it *corpus delicti*? I never could figure out which one is proper," asks C. Alvin.

"That's easy, kid," says Buster. "*Habeas corpus* is a legal mechanism to end the detention of a suspect, and *corpus delicti* is a legal term meaning body of the crime. My guess is either one used here is proper. So whatever you were going to say to him, I don't think he'll have any objections. Be my guest; say it and be done with it."

"In that case," says C. Alvin, smiling broadly, "goodbye Mr. Chips."

"I smell something strange," says George Kucor, another agent, jerking his head around and sniffing the room.

"By George, it could be from a transformer to run the toy trains," says Buster. "They can overheat and give off a strange odor, like rubber burning."

"No, Chief, I smell kerosene or gasoline," George says, dropping to the floor and looking under the platform. "Hey, chief, you're not going to believe what I found."

"Let me decide whether or not to believe you. What in the hell did you find?" asks the Chief.

"There's a can of lighter fluid under the platform," says George, "and the cuffs of his pants are wet, with a wire connected to a battery and timer set to go off at 12 o'clock. We got here just in time. An hour later, this place would be on fire."

"Are you shitting me?" asks the Chief.

"Chief, I swear on the grave of my father, by George."

Buster shakes his head, pauses a long time and shouts angrily, "Pass the word to check every nook and cranny in this fuckin' place for timers and explosives."

"He probably planned to go down in a blaze of glory," says C. Alvin.

"Don't jump to any conclusions yet," says Buster. "There may be other people involved or he may have suffered a heart attack. Suppositions drive me crazy."

"The coroner will find the cause of death," says C. Alvin.

"I know that, bug wit," says Buster. "Don't you think I know that?"

"Chief, if you have no objections," says Charlie, interrupting the battle of words, "I'll package and label the model freight car with this 'pale-green oatmeal,' that looks and smells like cow dung from Schwann Farm up the road."

"Do it, kid," says Buster, somewhat relieved that the task force is in complete control of the investigation. "We cannot afford to overlook anything that may be considered as evidence."

A few minutes later C. Alvin answers the telephone and speaks to the butler, calling to see if Mr. Rook is feeling better. He is shocked to learn that Rook was found slumping over the platform of his model trains, with one hand inside a bag of chips. "Funny," says the butler, "I never saw Master Rook eating tortilla chips. In fact, I never ever saw a bag of them inside the pantry."

After ending his conversation with the butler, C. Alvin turns around to find Buster starring out a window, watching the torrential rain outside. "You coming, Chief," he says. "I think our work is finished here."

"Our work is never finished, especially here," says Buster, frustrated and feeling the impact of finding another corpse when he was about to serve an arrest warrant. "Round up the boys and tell them to return to the *barn.* I'll wait here until the coroner comes to pick up Rook."

He continues to gaze through the window panes as the wind blows the rain against that side of the house. It's a pause to catch his breath and a moment of contemplation. "That poor bastard had the world in his hands," he says cynically to himself as the lighting seems to strike closer to this side of the mansion. Raindrops dribbling down the window panes reflect onto his cheeks and give the illusion of tears streaming down his face. "All those millions he made from the dot-com boom could have been put to a better use than resorting to revenge against Mark Hopkins. What a waste of money and a life that could have been better than it was. He'll probably go down in the history books as *The Avenger of Lone Pine.*"

Just as he completes his last word, a colossal thunderbolt strikes the pole barn about two hundred yards away from the mansion, causing flames to erupt in the loft full of hay. Buster speed dials 911 and within fifteen minutes a crew of firefighters can do nothing but watch the blaze and prevent it from spreading to other areas of the farm. A next door neighbor rushes over on horseback and when he finds buster talking to the fire chief, he tells them, "I saw the flames and immediately wanted to know if his thoroughbreds were safe. Often in a thunderstorm they will head to the pole barn for protection."

"I haven't a clue," Buster says, using both hands to cup his ears so he can hear the neighbor's conversation. "With very little moonlight and in this downpour, I can see or hear nothing except the crackling flames shooting high in the air over the pole barn. Everything inside will soon be reduced to ashes."

Fifteen minutes later, after getting a sign from the fire chief that the fire is extinguished, Buster returns to the back door of the mansion and hears a dog barking along with some commotion coming from the knoll area. When he cups his hands as if they are binoculars, he sees in the distance several stallions and a German shepherd frolicking around the base of the lone pine. "God has seen fit to save his stallions," he says, no longer feeling aggrieved. "Too bad, Rook didn't see fit to save himself. The windmills of his demented mind have ceased to turn."

Chapter 11

About a week later, on the seventh of June, the coroner, Dr. Youish, telephones Buster and asks, "Do you know what day this is?"

"Yes, Doc, I remember what happened on June 7th 1941," says Buster, "and the surprise attack on Pearl Harbor. Are you making a surprise attack with news about the death of Les Rook?"

"Les Rook did not suffer a heart attack," he tells Buster. "He died from guacamole, laced with arsenic, found in the toy freight car. I'm not supposed to comment, but off the record, that dip is what I call one *helluva* concoction of *snappy-peppy* hot-chili and cayenne sauce!"

"What you say is true," says Buster, dejectedly, "but it shows the weak, dark side, ah, the underbelly of America."

A few hours later as Buster is jotting down a few notes on a pad, he tells C. Alvin, "Les Rook was a mysterious man; a multimillionaire with the world in his hands who resorted to conspiracy by hiring thugs to do his dirty work and sabotage the mill. How stupid can he be by taking revenge against a former SEAL who risked his life in combat to keep the enemy away from our doorstep?"

"Obviously Rook was blinded by vengeance but not blinded enough to make millions in the dot-com boom," says C. Alvin. "Getting back to those chemicals under the display platform of his model trains, Les Rook probably wanted to use the fire as a cover-up of his suicide so as not to complicate his legacy. It's incredible how a mind can get all twisted and warped under severe pressure."

"We should find out where the leak came from inside the Bureau," says Buster. "Someone surely must have tipped him off that we were closing in on him and he decided suicide was not only his easy way out, it was his only way out."

"I'd like to believe that no one tipped him off, at least from inside the Bureau," says C. Alvin. "He was well-connected and knew he was trapped. His death will save the government some bucks by avoiding a nasty trial linking him to the union and his vengeance against Mark for his son's court-martial. Nothing good would come out of that mess, which would be embarrassing to the military."

When Mike Bloomburg is brought up to date by a telephone call from Mark and informed of Rook's death, he tells his partner, Lola, "It's a pity we are deprived of dragging Les Rook into court and exposing him to public ridicule."

"In the days of the old west," says Lola, sitting across from him inside her office at Mount Vernon Place, "when someone was suspected of committing a crime, such as stealing another man's horse, townspeople resorted to vigilante justice; they lassoed and hung the suspect on the nearest tree without a trial."

She leans back in her swivel chair and spins it 45 degrees to look at a painting hanging on the wall of her office; it's a masterpiece, painted by John Mulvany in 1876, titled: Preliminary *Trial of a Horse Thief–Scene in a Western Justice's Court.*

"You have a habit of studying that painting whenever we get involved in a criminal case," says Mike.

"True" says Lola. "It reminds me of the importance of a lawyer, judge and jury. In 1876 in St. Louis where this trial occurred, the artist left us with a historical record that represented a major change in the criminal justice system; whereby someone charged with having done something illegal, wrong, or undesirable was entitled to be represented by a lawyer, with proceedings ruled over by a judge and a verdict rendered by a jury."

Preliminary Trial of a Horse Thief–Scene in a Western Justice's Court, c. 1876, by John Mulvany (American 1844-1906).

Four weeks later, Buster and his JTTF team along with Mike Bloomburg spend most of their time with the District Attorney of Baltimore City. Together they develop a criminal case of sabotage, terrorism and possible murder. As the long hours begins to take a heavy toll on Mike, Lola helps by supplying vital information about the inner workings of the mill, especially the security personnel and procedures. Much of the information collected will also be beneficial in a subsequent civil case against the estate of Les Rook and the union regarding monetary damages to the mill; because the mill did not have insurance covering acts of terrorism or sabotage, BS is determined to seek reimbursement from the union who forced the mill to hire the accused in the first place, and from Les Rook, who planned the sabotage.

On the morning of the first day of August, also the first day of arraignment in the hall of the Criminal Court Building in downtown Baltimore, Franz Beckenbauer taps Mike Bloomburg on the shoulder. "It's important," he tells him, blocking his path.

"So is this arraignment," Mike answers, turning away abruptly and holding the door open for Lola, who is wearing a custom-tailored suit and jacket that accents her pregnancy.

"Pardon me, Mike, but perhaps you haven't heard the latest news," says Beckenbauer. "Moments ago in the holding cell of the court house the prosecutor reached a plea bargain with the two union suspects. They are willing to plead guilty to their crime, attach no blame or implicate anyone in the union and agree to a sentence for twenty years in prison without parole."

"That is good news," Mike replies and apologizes for his rudeness. "I was worried that the sabotage may be the result of terrorists. The plea bargain will save the government a ton of money and give us more time to devote to the civil case against Rook for damages to Bethlehem Steel."

"Is it your contention that based on your alliance with the DA that the elder Rook was out for revenge against Mark?" asks Franz.

"Resentment and recrimination too, but only old Rook can confirm it," says Mike. "Mark told me that his son may have had a problem with Signal Detection Theory (SDT)."

"I never heard about SDT," says Franz.

"You're not alone. Obviously both father and son could have benefited from a visit to a psychologist, who might explain how people make their decisions. It assumes that the decision-maker is not a passive receiver of information, but an active decision-maker who has to make difficult perceptual decisions under conditions of uncertainty and stress. The receptor inside Rook's son saw an opportunity for power and money and the receptor inside old man Rook saw revenge when Mark helped to uncover the sabotage at Edgewood Arsenal. When we get to court for the civil case, you'll hear a better explanation from our psychiatrist who will testify about their SDT."

"Maybe it has something to do with their DNA, too," says Franz. "In the meantime you have my assurance that the union will make good on your claims of liability. Hope you won't put us out of business altogether."

After Mike Bloomburg hears the defendants plead guilty in the courtroom, he is handed a citation in which the family of Captain Jones has filed suit against Bethlehem Steel for negligence in failing to have safety procedures to override the computerized shutdown and safer pathways in the mill for employees to escape from such a catastrophe.

Later that night, when Mike visits Mark at his home to give him the news of the latest lawsuit, Mark tells him to settle the suit as quickly as he can. "We are a family of workers at the mill," he says sincerely, kissing a framed photo of his father that he lifted off the top of the baby grand.

"It's the right thing to do, something my father would do if he were standing here," says Mark, "and as painful as it is for Capt. Jones' family, no amount of money will bring him back to life. The sooner we put this tragedy behind us, the better for everyone concerned. The country is in a bleak period and the disaster at the mill couldn't have come at a worse time. If this was God's will, it is unjust since BS was doing its best to find jobs for workers when other firms are cutting back and furloughing people."

After Mark excuses himself to answer a call on his cell, Lola motions for Mike to come into their study. She explains that the long hours at Mount Vernon Place are over since she is only a month away from her due date. "I've told you many times that your pregnancy takes precedence over all work at Mount Vernon," says Mike, "but you never complained and always told me to 'table it.' I should have been more insistent, but didn't want to complicate things. Although you have a nanny and Mark's mother to help out, the needs of Jaime and Baby Ruth are becoming stressful."

"I'm worried that they have developed a dripping nose and slight fever," she tells him. "The doctor said it could be the flu and contagious, a dangerous situation since I'm so close to my countdown. Looking out for 5-year old Jaime and 3-year old Baby Ruth is getting to be more than I can handle. Then add the complications from the explosion at the mill, which means, Mark will be needed there instead of being here with me."

"If you need anything, dial M for Mike," he tells her, dating himself by remembering the old rotary dial on a telephone. "What bothers me more is watching Mark's resolve to make the mill better than before. He's trying to *outdo* his father and grandfather. He doesn't realize he has good people who can make it easier."

"You can't blame him, can you?"

"As they say in litigations," says Mike, "when the dust settles, there may be a rainbow with a pot of gold for BS. It's not a case of whether or not we'll win, but how much money is awarded in a judgment. Whatever we get in monetary damages will give him enough funds to streamline his production line. Furthermore, the Wew twins will surely have some good ideas for an upgrade. You have to remind him, he still has his best people around him."

For several months Mark has been dwelling on the huge profit he made from the sale of the Remington bronze and came to the conclusion that he should share it with the WEN thrift store.

“”I have a bit of news for you, Miss Turtledove,” he tells her, dropping in unexpectedly on a bright Saturday afternoon. “You’ll have a new owner of your building, starting today.”

“Oh no,” she answers quickly. “That usually means the new landlord makes a small improvement and increases the rent.”

“Your new landlord will make whatever improvements you feel are needed, but with no increase in rent,” says Mark. “In fact, you won’t have to pay anyone rent anymore. I’ve bought the building and am the new owner, at least temporarily.”

“What do you mean by temporarily?”

“Perhaps you better have a seat.”

Mark takes her by the hand over to a stool behind the counter and continues his conversation. “It’s important to support good causes like WIN, so here’s the deal: At the end of five years, if you or whoever is running your branch of WIN is still in business here, the building will be yours. We only have to sign a Deed of Partnership and that will be drawn up by my attorney next week.”

“I don’t believe it. I mean I believe you, but don’t believe that someone would make such a proposition. Would you mind if I locked the store and invited you upstairs for a snack in my apartment?” she says with tears running down her cheeks.

Chapter 12

On Labor Day Lola is rushed to the hospital and delivers twin boys, each weighing five pounds five ounces. Dr. Bruce Rolf, the obstetrician at Sinai Hospital tells Mark, pacing in the hallway, "The first was delivered head first and the second seven minutes later, born breech. Mother and babies are doing well."

"Twin boys?" asks Mark, suddenly feeling lightheaded. "We decided not to ask anything about her pregnancy, although I was marking off the weeks, which came to 37. It never occurred to us that two boys were on the way."

An hour later Mark is comforting his wife who is just as surprised as him and tells him, "Let's name them 'Francis Key' Hopkins and 'Scott Key' Hopkins, after Francis Scott Key, author of America's national anthem, *The Star Spangled Banner*."

"Dr. Rolf told me," Mark says to his wife, "I could swear they were both smiling just before I gave them a slight pat on their back and began crying. I mean they began crying, not me."

A few days later when Mark checks his emails, he finds one from Monty Montgomery, one of his former SEALS, living in Venice, California. He begins by congratulating them on the birth of their twins and asks Mark to phone him when he's not too busy changing diapers. "It's about an upcoming auction with some art available that would require some research. If my hunch is right, it will be worth the effort but you have to act now," he writes.

After bouncing it around in his mind for an hour or two, he phones Abigail to see if she can participate on a conference call with Monty. "It may entice you out of retirement if Monty's hunch is right about some art being auctioned in LA," Mark tells her. "I can think of no one better than you for the job and if it pans out, you are obligated to no one except Monty Montgomery, the tipster who deserves a finder's fee."

"Interesting," Abigail says, pronouncing it slowly in four syllables, "and even if it doesn't *pan* out, it might be a chapter worth including in my book. It's not the monetary value, but I am still driven by an inner force, almost like an addiction, to take on a new challenge. Let's not waste any time. Get us connected to Monty in southern California."

Monty tells them on their subsequent conference call, "An old time movie star by the name of Rex Ingram died in 1969 and his second wife, Dena, recently died. I heard about her estate scheduled for auction and went to her home in Hollywood. The walls were loaded with paintings, all in carved-wood frames with Islamic inscriptions, but the paintings looked like copies by an amateur painter. It didn't make sense to me, but in the attic closets were a stack of beautiful paintings, all without frames. Do you know anything of Rex Ingram?"

"I do," says Abigail. "Besides being an old movie buff, I was an intern in Hagerstown in the late 1960's when he loaned the museum a painting of Islamic women with their faces tattooed. Once you saw it, you never forgot it. Rex was a very gifted African-American, recognized for his great acting talents but known to very few for collecting art."

"It's a small world. Seems you've made a connection to Monty," says Mark. "I'll hang up and let you two vultures do your picking together. I hear the twins crying and better help Lola before she gives me another scolding."

"That leaves just you and me on the line," says Abigail. "Go on."

"Her estate will be auctioned off next Friday in a tent behind her house," Monty explains. "According to a local auctioneer who has been called in for a quick sale, with no guarantees, meaning everything is sold as-is, where-is."

"That doesn't give me much time," says Abigail. "When can I have a look at the things?"

"You can't," says Monty. "The viewing is over with. You'll just have to come on Friday, the day of auction, and inspect everything as it's being sold."

"That complicates things," she says reluctantly. "It means I have no time to do any research."

"That's right," he says, "but it means everyone is in the same boat and has the same problem. From what Mark told me about you, you have good instincts. You'll need it, because you have to think and make your decision to buy instantaneously."

"I'll get back to you as soon as possible, Monty," she says, ending the conference call and leaning back in her swivel chair. "I wonder if Womble would join me on a flight to LA. At least it would be someone I could lean on for advice, just as I did at Ridgefield."

Four days later, Abigail and Womble are on a 4 pm American Airlines flight from BWI to LAX. "You can set your watch back three hours to 1:15 pm," says Abigail, opening her laptop computer. "I feel lucky with you along on this trip. Two keen minds are always better than one dancing in and out of retirement."

She hands the computer to Womble and says, "Have a look at this bio of Rex Ingram."

Womble leans back in his seat and changes the font size so it's easier to read: Rex Ingram was born on a houseboat on the Mississippi River near Cairo, Illinois, after his mother went into labor on her way home from visiting relatives in Natchez, Mississippi. His father was a riverboat fireman on the steamer *Robert E. Lee*. "Incredible!" says Womble. "From those humble beginnings, he became the first black man to earn a Phi Beta Kappa key at Northwestern Medical University. That's the same university that Lois Carnegie graduated from. Small world."

"Read on, maestro. The best is yet to come," she says, sipping a glass of champagne in her first-class seat.

Womble scrolls down and continues to read about Ingram attending a military school. "They don't say when or where, but that he was standing on a street corner in Hollywood when the director of *Tarzan of the Apes* asked him to audition in 1918. It doesn't say if he acted in plays at Northwestern, like Charlton Heston, or why he gave up medicine to go into acting."

"I've always been intrigued by the DNA of families," says Abigail. "How do you suppose his mother and father could produce such a remarkable son from such humble beginnings?"

"The same thing holds true for Leonard Bernstein," answers Womble. "His father was a mailman. I presume that talent is not always something automatically handed down through bloodlines like a thoroughbred horse. Somewhere along the way God must touch a person and lead him to a good and better life."

"Speaking of life," says Abigail, "I'd love to see your Ridgefield team develop a film of 'Two Spirits, Rex Ingram and Richard Wagner, Colliding over the Chesapeake Bay.' Think of it, art, medicine, music and drama involving two great characters of German and Muslim origins; ingredients that should arouse an audience. Don't let me interrupt you. Please continue reading. You're not even near the tip of the iceberg yet."

"To support himself," says Womble, "he took up boxing. *Ebony Magazine* called him 'the greatest Negro heavyweight prospect since Jack Johnson.' In 1933 he landed a role in the Gershwin production of "Porgy and Bess" on Broadway. Subsequently, because of racism and bigotry, he was denied roles. Of course, no one could blame him for refusing to accept any work that was demeaning to blacks. He was a man of principles, but that refusal kept him off the stage and below the radar screen of casting directors."

"You're about to come to the good part," she tells him.

"In 1940 he played the part of an enormous genie in the British film, "The Thief of Baghdad," which made him an international star. The film won three Academy Awards. In 1943 he appeared with Humphrey Bogart in *Sahara*. I remember him chasing a Nazi officer who tried to escape from a bunker; Rex chased him over sand dunes, tackled him like a linebacker and pushed his head into the sand to save the tank platoon that was guarding a waterhole."

"I didn't realize you were a movie buff."

"Oh no, in 1949 he pleaded guilty to transporting a 15-year-old white girl from Kansas across state lines for immoral purposes, a violation of the Mann Act. He served ten months of an eighteen-month sentence in jail and afterwards suffered bouts of depression. Incredible!"

"Why would a man of his intelligence and star-power do such a thing?" asks Abigail.

"Are you asking, 'Why would he kidnap a girl' or why would he plead guilty?'"

"I never thought of it that way but I'd like to know the answer to both questions," Abigail says, eager to get his opinion.

"I could give you ten answers to the first question. But I would venture to say that he pleaded guilty to spare the girl the publicity, embarrassment, slander and scorn of a protracted trial in the early days of television."

"I can imagine the prosecutor would love to put a black man on trial," says Abigail. "Racism was still prevalent throughout America."

"It goes on to mention," says Womble, "that this incident had a serious negative impact on his career for the next six years."

"A weaker person would probably commit suicide."

"Nevertheless," says Womble, "he regained his footing and in 1955, landed a role as a Sukulu Chieftain in *Tarzan's Hidden Jungle*. Rex was a survivor and, in 1960, appeared with Burt Lancaster in *Elmer Gantry*. In 1962, he became the first African-American actor to be hired for a role on a TV soap opera, *The Brighter Day*, but found it harder and harder to land a good role until Bill Cosby used his influence and got him a small part in *I Spy* in 1965 and *The Bill Cosby Show* in 1969, the year he died."

"What a career he had," says Abigail. "I remember that he was one of a few actors who played both God, in *The Green Pastures* in 1936, and the Devil, in *Cabin in the Sky,* directed by Vincente

Minnelli in 1943. And you're right; his life story would make a *helluva* movie, as you would say. But there is absolutely no mention of him being a collector of art."

Two days later, at 9:45 am, they are seated under a tent in the backyard of Ingram's deceased second wife's home in the Hollywood Hills.

"It's going to be a scorcher today, with temperatures expected to reach the high 90's," says Abigail.

"Are you referring to the temperatures outside or inside the tent? asks Womble.

"Inside for sure," she answers, growing edgy in anticipation of a bidding war to begin at 10:15.

"It's a crap shoot, kid," he tells her with a nudge of his elbow. "Trust your instincts and go for it. As I told you during our flight here, I'll back you and put up whatever you need, but please keep it under $100,000. Please."

"I spotted seven paintings by Etienne Dinet, a well-known French painter of Orientalist subjects that I'd like to bid on," says Abigail. "But I also spotted a Dutch dealer -- now based in Paris -- who must know about the Orientalist paintings, too. He's sitting in the first row on the other side of the center aisle."

"Just have your paddle ready and don't let him outbid you on anything you want," says Womble. "There won't be many opportunities to buy from a house sale like this one. Auction houses in Paris could probably guarantee the estate a higher price for Orientalist paintings."

"It just occurred to me," says Abigail, "that we should decide whether or not to bid on the best painting or buy one or two of lesser quality. Which way should we go?"

"I believe in leveraging my purchase and prefer to spread out the funds on two or more opportunities, rather than risk everything on one swing at the ball."

"I can live with that approach," she tells him.

"As Julius Caesar would say, let the games begin and let the chips fall wherever they may fall," says Womble.

Over the next two hours of fast selling, Abigail manages to buy four unframed paintings for $40,000, followed by three paintings which are beautifully framed with Islamic inscriptions, for $800 each. Her invoice shows a subtotal of $42,400, to which is added a 20 percent buyers premium of $8,480, which brings the grand total to $50,880. "If you want to take a plunge with me, your investment will be one-half of $51,880, which includes a finder's fee of $1,000 to Monty, for starters."

"That comes to $25,940, but what's 'for starters' mean?"

"We'll have to find a way for someone to help us pack them for our return flight tomorrow," she says, "then there will be cleaning and restoration charges to conservator Max Macher in Edesville."

"I don't know enough about art, but I accept your offer of a half-share of today's winnings," he says, unhesitatingly. "Those four unframed paintings, especially three of Algerian women with their faces covered with Islamic markings, send a chill up my spine. From what I've read, Islamic art is already popular with international collectors and primed for a boom among collectors in America, India and China. What puzzles me is why you bought three poorly-painted framed copies of the three unframed Orientalist paintings."

"You probably didn't realize that the copies, although of poor quality, had Islamic inscriptions carved into their wooden frames," says Abigail. "I wanted those frames because they were originally made for the three unframed paintings, if that makes any sense to you."

"Why would someone remove an original painting from its original frame and replace it with a poor amateurish copy?" asks Womble.

"I'm afraid that is a question that can only be answered by the deceased wife, who may have been a frustrated artist who switched the canvases and preferred to see her work hanging on the walls of her home instead of the originals painted by Etienne Dinet."

The following week Max Macher examines the first of the four unframed paintings on an easel in his conservation studio in Edesville, Maryland. "It could be covered with a heavy layer of nicotine," he tells Abigail, who drove two hours from her condo in Baltimore, "but hopefully it's over a heavy coat of old varnish. The former owners were suspected of being heavy cigarette-smokers."

He takes a long wooden stem, wraps a small amount of cotton around the tip and dips it into the first in a line of glass bottles containing solvents specially prepared with mixtures of naphthalene, acetone and a liquid soap cleaner; the percentages of each chemical additive is varied to produce the lowest, on the left, to the most-aggressive solvent, on the far right, to dissolve grime and varnish. In the upper right corner of the canvas, he rolls the stem over a one-inch square section of the canvas. When he examines the cotton swab, its color is a dirty yellow, similar to Dijon mustard. The square in the upper right has changed from a green to a blue sky. "I don't see any craqueleur or any lifting of pigment, so lining on new linen won't be necessary. I don't believe the artist painted in glazes, so 80 percent of the top layer of varnish can be removed with a light cleaning."

"Tell me about the artist," says Max, anxious to know as much as possible about his paintings.

"Etienne Dinet traveled from France to Algeria in 1884, settled in Bou-Saada and eventually converted to Islam," says Abigail. "Most of the paintings I've read about in auction catalogs and art reference books are works that he painted on linen."

"This is the first time I've cleaned one of his paintings and it's easy to see why he was collectable," says Max. "This one is beautifully composed and simplistic; an image that is easily remembered."

"Most of his paintings could be considered ethnographic because each one captures a particular image of Islamic society."

"They also have a distinct mauve coloring in the skin and clothing of the women." says Max. "When I was an apprentice in the conservation lab of a museum, I came to the conclusion that all the great painters, from Raphael to Rubens, Titian to Veronese, and Rembrandt to Vermeer had a distinct color that came only from a peculiar mix of minerals. It didn't come from tubes of paint bought in an artist's supply shop, even in the 16th century. It was their secret formula and many didn't keep a record of what minerals and percentages were ground up in a mortar with a pestle. It was like a cook who never needs a recipe."

"But here is a *horse* of a different color," says Abigail, handing him a 20 x 24-inch canvas depicting Arabian horses in flight across a desert. "Pardon my pun."

"Yes, this painting could have glazes mixed with varnish and will require a different cleaning of the old top layer," says Max. "It doesn't seem to have the nicotine and grime."

"The owner probably had it stored in an attic, where it would not have been exposed to smoke from cigars, cigarettes and pipes," says Abigail. "This one is painted by Alfred deDreux (1810-1860), a court painter for Louis Napoleon III. One of his paintings is for sale in a prestigious London gallery with a price tag of $750,000."

"Is that right?" asks Max, shaking his head. "I wonder what the price would be if we weren't in a worldwide recession."

"That painting was one of his masterpieces and only four-feet high by three-feet wide, with two young girls picnicking in a forest with their stallions grazing nearby," boasts Abigail. "DeDreux was always held in esteem by collectors of sporting art, whereas Dinet was acclaimed as a painter of Orientalist art."

After carefully measuring the cubic-centimeters of several solvents, Max creates a cleaning solution that has a viscosity similar to clear dish-liquid soap. Again he takes a cotton swab, dips it into the solution and presses it against the inside surface of the rim to remove some excess and rolls it in a one-inch square in the upper right corner of the canvas. A yellowish-green layer comes off onto the cotton swab, producing a blue sky in the upper right corner. "These are the moments that are the most enjoyable for me as a conservator," he says, smiling broadly. "It's exciting to clean a painting and restore it to its original state."

"Time is not of the essence," Abigail tells him. "Take your time and do the best you can for me. I can wait at least two months to see the results, no matter how long it takes. Please take some photos of 'before and after' so I can show my partner the fruits of your labor."

"I'll get the job done on time, no matter how long it takes," says Max, wobbling his head and blushing about the meaning of those words, "and what about the other three paintings that are framed?"

"Remove the canvas and only clean the frame," says Abigail. "Those carved frames are very valuable and will fit my unframed paintings."

"What do you want me to do after I clean the frames?" asks Max.

"You can frame my original Dinet paintings in those frames," says Abigail. "The idea of an artist removing a great original and substituting her copy is intriguing and may be something to consider later for a film segment or short story."

A week before Christmas, Abigail drives on cold winter roads with occasional snow flurries from Baltimore to Edesville to pick up the paintings from the Ingram estate that have been restored by Max Macher. After she follows him into his studio, they are resting on a row of four easels carefully arranged for her viewing. The exhibition stuns Abigail; her legs weaken and Max, anticipating her reaction, quickly moves a chair behind her knees so she can sit and digest everything.

"This is somewhat of a shock because I just saw flashes back to their earlier condition, covered with nicotine, grime and old varnish," says Abigail, putting her hand over her heart to feel an increased heartbeat. "But all that is gone now and each one is radiating with the high workmanship of Dinet and DeDreux."

"Consider it a Christmas present from the artist to you for deciding to restore his paintings to their original condition," says Max.

"This is the best present I've ever received," she says. "I've been around art for over 40 years and maybe it affects me differently now because I am moving from curator to director to collector. But as they say, 'scratch a collector and you'll find a dealer underneath.' At my age, when you're risking a good portion of your life savings to invest in art, the angst is definitely different. I'm floored. Would you leave me alone for a few minutes, please?"

Her eyes become teary, knowing that Monty's hunch about the Ingram estate and her decision to take Womble along for his support may pay big dividends later on. "We mustn't forget to send Monty a larger finder's fee," she reminds herself.

During the long drive back to Baltimore, Abigail spends the entire time dwelling over her next steps. With her cell mounted on the dashboard, she manages to track down Womble and arranges for him to meet her at her condo the following afternoon. Together they decide that each will chose a painting to keep and put the two remaining ones into an auction of Nineteenth Century Paintings in New York, in a spring sale around the end of May.

Womble tells her, "It's like having your cake and eating it, too."

"Santa Claus has come early to my condo and hung a beautiful painting over my artificial fireplace."

"Your fireplace may be artificial, but that Dinet painting is far from it," boasts Womble. "Being around you has been and will always be exciting. Lately I've learned in a very short time something special about dealing in art. Let's keep our partnership active and use whatever money we get from the auction for further investments in art."

"You're hiding something from me, aren't you?" asks Abigail, perceptively.

"I tried to hide it from everyone but sooner or later the truth will win out," says Womble, with despair in his voice. "It's called age-related macular degeneration (AMD), a medical condition which usually affects older adults."

"Don't tell me you have AMD?" asks Abigail.

"During the past month," says Womble, "an exam by doctors at Hopkins showed the beginnings of a loss of vision in the center of the visual field, the macula, because of damage to my retina. It's in the early stages but will eventually make it difficult or impossible to read or recognize faces, although enough peripheral vision remains to allow other activities of my daily life."

"I can't believe it," says Abigail, shocked by his revelation. "I thought it strange the way you tossed your head around to get a good look at those paintings, but never suspected AMD."

"Keep it under your hat, please," says Womble. "You're the only one who knows about it."

CHAPTER 13

It's the middle of February and a light snow falls as Little Ben Bender grips the wheel of his pickup truck for the two hour drive from Easton to Baltimore. After passing over the Chesapeake Bay Bridge, he turns to his son, sitting in the passenger seat next to him, and says, "Wouldn't you prefer to fly to Florida instead of taking Amtrak? It would mean you're there in about three hours versus 24."

"We've been through all that a dozen times, Dad," Chubby says. "As I tried to explain, I enjoy meeting new people on the train and seeing something different along the way. As long as I get there by tomorrow night, it's no big deal."

An hour later, Little Ben makes a left turn from Pratt Street onto Charles Street and notices that about five inches of snow has fallen, giving *Charm City* a special gleam. A few minutes later, Chubby points to the Washington Monument designed by Robert Mills on his left and says, "It was the nation's first monument, built in 1815, to honor George Washington, and stands 175 feet. But the people in Washington County claim that their memorial honoring our first president was started later but finished first; it's located on South Mountain close to the Appalachian Trail, off Route A-40."

"Spoken like a tour guide, son," says his father. "And on your right is the United Methodist Church, a grand Victorian-Gothic architectural marvel that was built in 1872 on the former site of the home of Charles Howard, husband of Elizabeth Phoebe Key, daughter of Francis Scott Key, author of "*The Star Spangled Banner*," who died there. I've been studying up on *Balamer* since you signed with the *Oryuls*."

Little Ben finally pulls his truck into a small cutaway lane for dropping off passengers at Penn Station. As he hands Chubby his suitcase, his father checks the time on his wrist watch. "It's 1:30," his father tells him, "and you have 30 minutes to board your train, so don't go flirting or goofing off with the girls on the way to your track. You'll have plenty of time to fool around with the girls in Florida where it's a *helluva* lot warmer than around here. Remember to call me after you check into your hotel in Sarasota."

"I heard you the first time, Dad, and four times afterward while you were driving from Easton," says Chubby, laughing. "It's not the first time I'm reporting for spring training with the O's. Stop worrying. I can take care of myself as long as my knuckleball flutters."

Chubby gives his father a big hug and disappears through the shiny brass doors of Penn Station. Once inside the terminal, he is focused on his mission and walks casually to the center of the terminal as if it were game-time and his manager called him in from the bullpen in the ninth inning with the bases loaded, two outs. Chubby is blessed with confidence and the resolve to concentrate on everything that's happening now. He studies the giant AMTRAK electronic board that shows the departure and arrival information and notes the track number for the *Silver Star*. As he approaches an escalator, he notices two girls, giving him the eye.

"I hope you're going my way," he says. "Can I help you with your baggage?"

"Only if you're catching a train to Philly," they tell him in unison.

"Sorry, but I'm heading south where girls like you wear a bikini, not bundled up in a fleece jacket," he says. "I'll catch you in April on my way back to *Balamer*, so keep your motors running till then."

A few minutes later he puts his suitcase into a sleeper compartment as the conductor shouts 'All Aboard, *next-a* station, Washington.'

The sound of the conductor's voice and the jolt of the wheels of the locomotive beginning to move send jitters up his spine. Although he has been thinking about this moment all winter long, he's finally reporting voluntarily with pitchers and catchers for the start of spring training in Sarasota, Florida.

After the train enters an underground tunnel, his compartment turns almost pitch-black, except for a dim light overhead. He leans his head against the cold window to cool his forehead and closes his eyes as a series of quick flashbacks cross his mind. "My rookie season in the big leagues is over," he tells himself. "I have to forget about a sophomore jinx, be more aggressive and go after the hitters. If I can improve on my command of the knuckleball and changeup, last year's strikeouts-to-walks ratio of 4.0 K/BB and record of 10 and 5 with an ERA of 0.495 will be ancient history, exactly what Jim Honochick told me during our winter workouts at Ridgefield."

About an hour later the train makes a brief stop in Washington DC, and Chubby catches a glimpse of young girls all bundled up for the winter snow that has hit the nation's capital. The conductor walks through his car and shouts in clear, distinct syllables, "*Next-a-sta-tion, Rich-mond, Vir-gin-i-a, y'all.*"

As the train continues its southward direction through another underground tunnel, he reflects again on his father's lessons pounded into him during the drive to Baltimore: "Work hard and you'll have a good year. Forget about a sophomore jinx. You've been training all winter to keep your body in the best physical shape possible. Each time you go to the mound as a relief pitcher and take the ball from the manager, stay aggressive and go after those batters at the plate. Think about those tough workouts at Ridgefield; throwing off the pitching mound inside the indoor batting cage and jogging on the beach in all kinds of weather."

At 3:30 pm, he is enjoying a lunch inside the dining car and carrying on a conversation with Acela Lori, an attractive 21-year old blonde, who just graduated from McDaniel College, formerly Western Maryland College, in Westminster.

"People from Baltimore call it *Westminister*, which always makes me laugh," she says. "It was blowing snow all over Westminster, worse than around the depot in Washington."

"I can tell right away that you're not from *Balamer*," he says.

"No, I'm from Charlotte, North Carolina and can't wait to get back home for a good night's sleep and some of mom's southern-fried chicken."

"And then what?" he asks.

"I'd like to go to graduate school for a master's in psychology if a scholarship is offered. My grades were almost *summa cum laude*, but it will take a miracle because all universities and colleges are cutting back on everything." She quickly types into her laptop computer and spins it around so he can read what she just typed: 'Tell me something about you.'

"First, you should know, I never could get my fingers to hit exactly in the center of the letter on a laptop keyboard," he says. "My fingers are too big and I'm always overlapping."

"Forget the keyboard," says Acela. "Talk as if I were taking your deposition in a court case."

"Oh shit, pardon my language," he says apologetically.

"Nothing to worry about," she says. "Everything's off the record."

During the next ten minutes he talks freely about baseball. He explains his workouts at Ridgefield, getting a tryout with the *Islanders*, and some of the crucial games he won and lost in two seasons with the Orioles; one as a rookie in the minor leagues and one as a big leaguer. When Acela switches subjects and asks about his life outside of baseball, he's somewhat embarrassed, but with her persistence, admits reluctantly to enjoying the quiet life on his father's farm in Easton and his two years at Chesapeake College in Wye, Maryland. He says everything in a Will Rogers style: No bravado, sprinkled with touches of humor and wit.

Her body language gives him the impression that she may be cautiously smitten. "I'm curious about your last name," he says. "Doesn't Amtrak have an Acela Express between Washington and Boston?"

'Funny you should mention it," she says, "because that's how I got my name. I was born inside a sleeper aboard an Acela Express and it caused all sorts of problems on my birth certificate. My mother and father couldn't decide my place of birth; one said it was in Washington DC and the other said it was over the border in Maryland. So they compromised and put down the name of the train, so I was born in Acela, Maryland, even though there's no such place. At least that's what they told me."

"I'll bet that it's the first time a baby girl was named after an express train," he says, laughing.

Over the next fifteen minutes it's Acela's turn to talk about herself; she's a psychology major who handles her laptop the way Jascha Heifetz plays his Stradivarius. After finishing a quick bio, she spins it around and shows him a photo of the Orioles taken last year, with a red circle around his head. For the next hour she's showing him how to create greeting cards that he can send to friends and fans over the Internet. After a long pause, she surprises him by saying, "I only have about an hour before we reach Charlotte. Let's play a guessing game; for each wrong answer, the loser has to remove an item of clothing."

"You must be good at it. Otherwise you wouldn't suggest such a crazy game."

"When it gets too risqué, we can call time out and bring in a relief pitcher from the bullpen," she tells him brazenly.

"You've picked up the lingo faster than the high-speed train you're named after."

"What was the song or tune that Nero fiddled while Rome burned?" Acela asks, smiling broadly

"*I'll See You in My Dreams*," answers Chubby, "or maybe it was '*Meet Me Tonight in Dreamland*."

"You only get one guess each time. Anyway both were wrong," says Acela. "Please remove your shirt."

"Now, for my question: Which answer is correct; Two and two is five, two and two equals five, or two and two makes five?'"

"None of them are correct," Acela says, laughing. "Now, I'll ask you again about the song that Nero played. You have to give me the right answer before I can ask a new question."

"I've got it this time. It's 'I don't want to set the world on fire, I just want to start a flame in your heart.'"

"Wrong again," she says, motioning for him to remove something else.

He takes off his wrist watch and drops it into a glass of water. "It's a Timex and keeps on ticking," says Chubby. "If I forget to take it with me, you can have it as a memento of our trip. Whenever it's twelve o'clock and the big hand, that's me, meets the little hand, that's you, think about me. I heard the conductor call out, '*next-a-sta-tion, Char-lot-ta*.'"

"10:30 pm. We're on time," she says, looking at his watch.

He carries her two suitcases off the train and gives her a warm embrace and gentle kiss, saying, "This has to last us until the next time we meet."

"This could be the start of a beautiful friendship," she says.

That night Chubby tosses and turns in his sleeper compartment. He's suddenly developed a toothache that is not excruciating but is just painful enough to keep him awake all night.

Around three in the afternoon his train finally pulls into Tampa and Chubby is still feeling some pain from his toothache as he boards a shuttle bus for the final two-hour link to Sarasota. Along the way he's trying to decide whether to report to Ed Smith Stadium or find a dentist. After arriving at the central bus terminal of Sarasota, he tells the cabby to take him to a good dentist.

"A good dentist?" asks the cabby, in a Yiddish émigré's accent. "A good dentist in Sarasota you won't find. They're all in Brooklyn. You want I should pull it myself?"

"Not if you don't have a license."

"You need a license to pull a tooth?" he asks quizzically. "I don't even have a driver's license."

"I assume you're kidding, so take me to the ballpark and step on it," says Chubby, trying to imitate the cabby's accent. "My toothache is getting worse just listening to your repartee."

"Listen, buddy, I don't know what *repartee* means, but they *aint gonna* fix no toothache at the ballpark. Still if *dats* where you *wanna* go, you'll be there in less than 10 minutes."

"It's a *helluva* way to start spring training, but the trainer should know a good dentist for me," says Chubby, glancing out at the bright sunshine and feeling the warm breeze of the Orioles spring-training camp.

After entering the clubhouse at Ed Smith Stadium, Chubby is greeted by the trainer, Pappy Kurall, who hands him his uniform with the number 13 woven on the backside. When he fails to say anything to him, Pappy realizes that something is wrong. "What's up, kid?" he asks.

Chubby tries to speak but his words are garbled. It's as if he is gargling with a mouthwash. By the painful look on his face with a swollen cheek, Pappy realizes that he has a severe toothache.

"I'll put the uniform in your locker, kid," says Pappy. "You can try it on tomorrow. It's already 5 and we should take care of your tooth first. I'll call a taxi and have the driver take you to our team dentist."

Chubby motions with his hands to indicate it's a molar. He writes on a pad that the toothache kept him awake all night and sapped his strength. His legs are beginning to feel wobbly.

"I can give you something to keep in your mouth around the tooth that will numb the gum a little," Pappy tells him. He finds a pint bottle of whiskey hidden behind some jockstraps in the back corner of the top shelf of his locker and uses the bottle top to pour out a shot. "Whatever you do, try to keep it around the bad tooth and don't swallow it."

Five minutes later Chubby hops out of the cab and slams the door shut as a maintenance man is hosing down the sidewalk in front of the dentist's office. He is about to walk down three steps leading into the entranceway to the building when he notices an attractive girl walking nearby. Instead of watching the steps in front of him, he turns to admire the short skirt that covers half of her thighs. A second later he plunges face forward, onto the concrete slab. To brace his fall, he extends both hands awkwardly, spitting out the whiskey and crying out for help. A passerby manages to get him to his feet and takes him inside the dentist office.

"Since you're already here," says the dentist, "I'll bundle an ice pack around your wrist to keep the swelling down and treat your toothache. I'll only need 15 to 20 minutes unless you need a root canal. In the meantime my receptionist will make arrangements to get you to the hospital where an orthopedist will examine your wrist."

Around noon, Chubby is resting in a private room at the hospital when the team doctor introduces himself. "I am Dr. Blaine and will try to keep my diagnosis as plain and simple as possible. The swelling has gone down, but the injury is much more than a sprain. The results of the x-rays and Magnetic Resonance Imaging (MRI) show that your wrist joints which include the carpal tunnel, anatomical snuffbox, flexor retinaculum, and the extensor retinaculum are severely damaged."

"That may be plain to you but not simple to me," says Chubby, puzzled and under sedation. "Can you run that by me again, Doc, in language I can understand?"

"To put it bluntly," says Dr. Blaine, "the ligaments in your wrist are severely damaged and you'll need an operation as soon as possible."

"My career is at stake here, Doc," says Chubby, with tears beginning to form in his eyes and words of despair slowly coming out of his mouth. "I was looking forward to spring training, not seeing my life go down the toilet. What should I do?"

"In situations like this one, we always get a second opinion. With your permission, I can send all the X-rays and MRI data electronically to Dr. James Andrews in Birmingham, Alabama."

"Who's he?"

"He's one of the most renowned orthopedic surgeons in the country, credited with saving the arms of many patients after they undergo his Tommy John Surgery. If I needed a second opinion and operation, Dr. Andrews would be my choice."

"Send everything to him, Doc," says Chubby, "I'm a pitcher with the Orioles. Will I be able to grip a baseball again?"

"I hope you can. Every team needs good pitchers, but the Orioles won't get it from Chubby Bender this season," says Dr. Blaine. "We've contacted Mr. Dunn who told us to do the best we can to take care of you. We'll keep you here another few days for further treatment and observation. You'll be getting a cast to protect your wrist this afternoon."

Each of the next three days Pappy knocks on his door at the hospital at 8:00 AM and 7:00 PM to see how he's feeling and answer any questions about training camp. They get along almost like a father and son, with Pappy kidding him when he learns that he was looking at a pretty girl instead of watching where he was walking. "Were you making a pitch at her, son?" asks Pappy. "If so, it was way outside and I wouldn't tell anyone about it."

On the fourth day, Dr. Blaine informs Chubby that Dr. Andrew's has confirmed the diagnosis of damage to his wrist joint and informed us that he cannot schedule you for an operation. "He's all booked up and his wife is having their sixth child," Dr. Blaine tells him. "Obviously, he's been busy in between his operations."

A month later, Chubby is back in Easton on his father's farm, continuing a prescribed rehabilitation program set up by Dr. Blaine, who performed the surgery himself to repair the ligaments in his wrist. At this point it's too early to say whether Chubby's career as a knuckleball pitcher is over. Certainly the injury is a big blow to his dreams of improving on his rookie season with the O's. Now, so much depends on factors beyond the surgery itself; factors such as the growth and reformation of tissue over the palmar and dorsal radiocarpal ligaments and the ulnar and radial collateral ligaments.

Although this is not the first time that an athlete suffered this kind of injury, the results are devastating to Chubby. All his life he's been an optimist and an independent, cocky guy, who did what he wanted to do when he wanted to do it. However, he's honest and blames no one except himself for losing sight of what he was supposed to be thinking and acting. Over and over again he asks himself, "Why me? Has God something else in mind at this stage of my life?"

When the major league season begins the first week of April, the *Orioles* undoubtedly feel the loss of a promising knuckleballer. After seven days on the road, the *O's* get off to a terrible start, losing their first five games, each by one run. But worse is the way they are throwing games away that they should have won easily. It seems as if they've forgotten the basic fundamentals. One of Chubby's teammates telephones him and says, "Our pitching is good but we're playing like zombies; forgetting everything that made us big leaguers. Wish you were here. Come back soon so you can give us a quick kick in the ass and get us back on track."

During the second week of the season, the *O's* are playing a little better but fail to hit in the clutch; outfielders neglect to call for a fly ball hit between them, and infielders stumble, letting routine foul balls bounce out of their gloves.

Around the third week of his rehabilitation, Little Ben joins his son on a long walk around his farm and encourages him to return to Chesapeake College, only a twenty-minute drive away by car. "You can enroll in an information technology course," he tells him. "Perhaps working at the computer will be a good exercise for your fingers and wrist. And between classes you can help your old baseball coach, Frank Szymanski and teach his pitchers how to throw a knuckleball. That doesn't mean stopping your rehabilitation program, but it will get your mind off the injury and put something worthwhile into your life. Your season as a knuckleballer is over for this year, but you're not crippled for life."

Chapter 14

Around the end of May, when Chubby's classes at Chesapeake College end, his father gets a telephone call from one of his buddies who served in Iraq with him. After the telephone call is completed, he tells his son, "That was Bigfoot Tavare, a Navajo Indian who was a medic with me in combat during the siege of Baghdad. I had promised to see him after we returned to the states and both of us got settled. He heard about you and wants you to come along and tell him if his son has the makings of a big leaguer."

"Where do they live and when do we go?" Chubby asks quickly. "The timing is good since school is over. I wouldn't know how to evaluate his son but I'll give it a try."

"Don't count yourself short, young man. Remember you were a part-time catcher with the *Skipjacks* at Chesapeake College a few years ago," Little Ben tells him. "They live on a reservation a few miles outside the town of Taos, New Mexico."

"Are we going to sleep in a teepee?" asks Chubby facetiously.

"You can sleep in one if it'll make you happy, but I assume that they'll have proper lodgings for us. I'll make reservations with Southwest Airlines. Their fares are the cheapest and bags fly free."

A few days later, at 9 am, both are flying at 30,000 feet from Baltimore's BWI to Albuquerque, New Mexico, and enjoying the hospitality of the stewardesses. After arrival, they transfer to a shuttle bus to Taos, with a brief stop in Santa Fe. Along the way Little Ben is on his cell with Bigfoot, giving him their arrival time at the Taos plaza. After meeting them in front of the Hotel La Fonda, Bigfoot drives his GMC pickup with over 150,000 miles on the odometer about three miles outside of town, on a road called Paseo del Norte, to a cluster of picturesque adobe houses. "The one with a slight pink sheen is mine," says Bigfoot. "We're all excited to have you here, amigos," he tells them, parking his pickup in front of his home. "Mi casa es su casa."

"Which means what?" says Little Ben.

"It's Spanish for 'My house is your house.' I could tell you in Navajo sign language and code but I don't want to confuse you on the first day you're here," says Bigfoot, laughing.

After everyone settles down and tastes a special sweet-squash, guacamole and cheddar-cheese dip smeared on Tex-Mex chips that Bigfoot's wife has prepared, Chubby is antsy to get outside and take a walk. "I can see that you both have a lot to catch up on, so if you don't mind, I'd like to stretch my legs. Where's your ballpark?" he asks.

"Let your ears point the way," says Bigfoot. "Kids will be yelling after every strike out or base hit. They play from dawn to dusk. There are never enough hours in the day."

Chubby meanders around the neighborhood for ten minutes, and then finds a regulation baseball field behind an adobe Spanish-revival-style schoolhouse. Chubby always enjoys watching batting practice but can't recall being on a field sprinkled with gravel instead of grass. One particular player taking infield practice catches his eye. He's a handsome catcher, who appears to be around 19 and stands about five-foot eight inches, with a build similar to Buster Cody, San Francisco Giants catcher. The old-time scouts would say, 'He has a *rifle* for an arm.'

"If I were a talent scout for the movies," Chubby tells him after he finishes taking infield and batting practice, "I'd take you to Hollywood and arrange for a screen test."

"Acting is not for me, but I've made a few bucks, posing with my grandfather's squash-blossom necklace for photographers and artists."

Chubby shakes his hand and says, "You've got big hands."

"Yes, I know."

"Really big hands," says Chubby, holding them about a foot apart.

"You must be Chubby Bender," says the catcher. "My father talked long hours about you. Your father helped to save his life when a mortar shell exploded near him in Iraq."

"So you are the son of Bigfoot Tavare?" asks Chubby, not paying much attention to what he said about his father saving his father's life in combat.

"Yes, I am Bighands Tavare."

"That name rings a bell; I mean, Tavare, not Two Bighands," says Chubby.

"You might be thinking of Jay Tavare. He's an actor and my uncle."

"Come to think of it, you also remind me of an outfielder for the Boston Red Sox, Jacoby Ellsbury, who blasted one of my knuckleballs over the Green Monster last year; it didn't win the game but the manager was ready to give me the boot. Ever heard of Ellsbury?"

"He's my cousin," Two Bighands says, laughing. "We're all related to one another on the reservation."

For the next four afternoons, Chubby is positioned behind home plate, watching Two Bighands' team in Taos play games against teams from Santa Fe and Albuquerque. He can't help noticing how he always makes contact with his bat, hitting towering bombs and low screamers, seventy percent of them over the fence for home runs. When his bat meets the ball, it has a peculiar cracking sound. "Of course," says Chubby to himself, "this is amateur competition, but from what I've seen so far, he has shown me some big-league-potential. And he's only 19."

When they walk around the reservation after dinner on the fourth day of consecutive games, Two Bighands tells Chubby, "I don't consider myself a home-run hitter. I just try to be consistent and make solid contact in front of the strike zone. The ball comes off my bat and next it's usually flying over the fence."

"My advice," says Chubby, "is to keep on doing whatever you're doing and don't let anyone try to change your approach. You have a God-given talent that is instinctive, intuitive, ah, and something that's goes beyond the nature of your swing. Although I'm not a scout or agent, I'd like to call Mr. Dunn and arrange for a tryout if you're willing to give everything you have to become a pro-baseball player."

"It's something I've had dreams about but didn't know how to follow," says Two Bighands. "Out here on the reservation, we can only call out to the spirits of our ancestors above to show us the way to a better life."

"From now on, leave everything to me," says Chubby. "Think of me as your interlocutor."

"I trust you know what you're doing."

At noon on the fifth day of his stay in Taos, Chubby makes a person-to-person call to Jack Dunn Jr. in Baltimore. "Where in the hell are you, Chubby?" asks Mr. Dunn. "We've been trying to get hold of you all week. Our lawyers want to take your deposition for a possible lawsuit against the owner of the building in Sarasota where you suffered your injury. We're trying to get back the fifty-grand it cost the club for your operation. When can you get your ass back to Sarasota?"

"I can take a plane tomorrow, provided you let me bring along a prospect that will bowl you over. I'll even pay his fare if you promise to give him a tryout, just like the one you gave me with the *Islanders* two years ago."

"What position does he play?"

"He's a catcher."

"Shit. You mean I have to go through all that stuff again?"

"It'll be worth it, Mr. Dunn, trust me," says Chubby. "He's the cousin of Jacoby Ellsbury and hits the ball harder than him. I feel obligated to you and the O's, who should have the first *crack* at him before I contact anyone else."

"Yea, yea, yea, kid," says Mr. Dunn. "Whatever it takes to get your ass in Sarasota as soon as possible is all right with me. Unless you hear otherwise in the next hour, take your prospect to Daytona Beach and see Joe Klein. I'm certain you remember him. I'll ask him to give your boy a tryout, but afterwards, get your ass in gear and contact our lawyers who are waiting to take your deposition."

"Why a deposition?"

"The owner of the building may be negligent for not having a handrail on the steps and pylons on the wet pavement," says Mr. Dunn.

The next day Two Bighands refuses to pack his bags until he can take Chubby for a ride around town in a buckboard pulled by a single horse. "There are no springs in the seat or cushions for your rear end," says Two Bighands. "From what I heard about relief pitchers, they all have a 'hard ass,' so it will be 'no sweat' for you, *ke-mo-sa-be.*"

They pass an adobe home with a sign that reads: 'Taos Art Museum.' Two Bighands says, "That was the home of Nicolai Fechin, a Russian born in Kazan who came here in 1929 to recuperate from tuberculosis. My grandfather posed for him and Fechin called him 'Navajo Joe,' but that wasn't his real name. People around the museum believe that it is one of Fechin's best paintings and sell prints of it, too."

"Very peaceful here with those mountains in the distance."

"They're the Taos Mountains," says Two Bighands.

"How did Taos get its name?"

"Our ancestors called it 'the place of the red willows.' We now have about 5,000 people living here. A few movie stars like Julia Roberts and Dennis Hopper spend time here as well."

"I thought Dennis Hopper was dead."

"His home is still here," says Two Bighands. "Some say his house is haunted because they see his spirit flying around inside. You'll have to come back again after you get me a job with the Orioles."

"I just hope Mr. Klein, Mr. Majeski and the *Islanders* will like the potential I see in you."

"Before we take off for Florida, there is someone special that I want you to meet," says Two Bighands, giving his horse a 'giddy-up,' which is similar to shifting the gearshift in the manual transmission of his father's truck from low to medium gear. A few minutes later Little Ben sits on a bolder in a remote section of Taos when a Medicine Man approaches Two Bighands. They exchange some Navajo signs. By their gestures, Chubby gets the impression that Two Bighands is asking the Medicine Man to bless Chubby's injured wrist and their upcoming trip to Florida. Chubby tells himself, "My boy just used his hands to mimic the jaws of an alligator opening and closing, just like those crazy *gator* fans of the University of Florida football team."

The Medicine Man turns his head upward and cries out a song to the spirits hovering over the reservation, then reaches into his pocket and removes a bundle of spices and herbs. He spits on Chubby's wrist, spreads them on the topside and ties them with a string of rawhide.

Chubby looks down at his wrist and says, "I know it's sacrilegious, but that bundle would make a nice seasoning for chicken soup."

Then the Medicine Man dances around Chubby six times; each time around, he gives a different war cry along with a pantomime of the six senses of a human being: to see, smell, touch, hear and taste plus one for common sense. Afterwards, Two Bighands stretches his arm outward until they rest on the Medicine Man's shoulders as a sign of appreciation, and motions Chubby to join them. "He's close to 90 and losing his eyesight but not his powers of healing," says Two Bighands.

"And what did he tell you?"

"He said that you will not feel any more pain in your wrist, but will have a pain in your ass if I don't get signed by the Orioles!"

On the five minute drive back to their adobe home, Chubby asks Two Bighands, "Would you mind answering a question that has been bothering me for a long time?"

"A long time?"

"Yes, ever since the first time I saw those John Ford westerns."

"O.K., what's the question?"

"Why do Navajos never knock before entering a wigwam or tipi other than their own?" asks Chubby, puzzled. "And how does a Navajo send a personal smoke signal to another in his wikiup without the whole tribe knowing about it?"

"You really want to know?"

"I really want to know," says Chubby.

"In the first place, Navajos never lived in wigwams; they lived in hogans, made from earth, and eventually in adobe houses like ours. Secondly, wigwams were used by the Ojibwa tribe, which is another story for another time. I don't want to tell you anything that will cloud your mind. We've got to think, eat and sleep baseball until I get that tryout."

Two days later, Chubby is introducing Two Bighands to general manager Joe Klein and manager Hank Majeski, Jr., who are sitting inside the clubhouse of the Daytona Beach *Islanders* at Jackie Robinson Stadium. "It seems like yesterday I was putting on a uniform and trying to win a spot in the lineup for you two buzzards," says Chubby, brazenly.

"The kid hasn't lost any of his nerve," Joe tells Hank.

"It goes with the makeup of a relief pitcher," says Majeski. "You sure made us proud the way you played in your rookie season, kid."

"We were all shook up when we heard about you breaking your wrist," says Mr. Klein. "We already have two catchers signed for the season, but Mr. Dunn said to give your boy a tryout, so we're giving him a tryout."

Over the next two hours, Tavare makes a good impression, especially on the manager. "At 19, he's way ahead of some of the players here, especially with his power and bat speed," says Majeski. "He has a compact swing and always seems to make good contact and I like the way he's patient and waits for a good pitch to hit. That's something that no one can teach a hitter. It's instinctive."

After having a drink of water at the dugout dispenser, they lean their heads together and begin whispering into each other's ears. Soon they both are nodding to one another. Finally Mr. Klein walks slowly over to Tavare and explains that, despite their reluctance to sign him, something tells them not to let him get away. They offer him a job as a bullpen catcher, which means he's on the injured reserve list. "You'll get a chance to play," says Majeski, butting in, "if and when one of our catchers is injured."

"It's a win-win situation for you and the Orioles," Klein tells him. "You'll be starting at the bottom and the O's might be the first pro team to sign a Navajo Indian catcher, even if he is only a rookie on the reserve squad."

A week later one of the *Islanders'* catchers is injured in a collision at home plate when he tries to block the plate with his left leg. It's diagnosed as torn cartilage in his knee, a season-ending injury, and a chance for Tavare to step in as a replacement.

During the next three weeks Two Bighands is a backup catcher, playing only once every five days. Eventually Al Calicomo, the best pitcher on his staff tells Majeski, "Tavare knows what he's doing behind the plate, always calls for the right pitch and gives us a good target with his mitt. All the guys trust him. You should make him the regular catcher, and I guarantee we'll move up in the standings. It's also fun to watch him blast those balls *outta* the park."

Wanting to keep his pitching staff happy, Hank always talks things over with bullpen coach Rick Dempsey before making any decisions about his pitchers. When he hands the lineup card to the ump at the start of the next game, Tavare's name is listed as catcher and eighth batter in the *Islander*s starting lineup. "My bullpen coach tells me it's time to test our wonder-boy catcher by playing him until he drops dead or his batting average sinks to his playing weight, whichever is first," Majeski tells the umpiring crew.

Although it's the middle of the season, Tavare makes the most of his opportunity to play every day and literally tears the cover off the ball, ending the season with a .280 batting average and 25 screaming homers.

When Klein hosts a party for the team after the last game of the season, Majeski tells him, "*The Islanders* pitching staff improved their combined ERA and gives Tavare most of the credit for the way he was able to get them to relax when things got rough; they also said something that I wasn't paying much attention to during the last half of the season."

"What was that?" asks Klein.

"I wasn't privy to what was said between the pitcher and catcher during a game," says Majeski, "but apparently Tavare taught our pitchers some coded words in the Navajo language. They were having fun, cursing the umpire when he called a pitch a 'ball' instead of a 'strike,' or a runner 'safe' instead of 'out.' Now I know why they never covered their mouth with their glove when they had those conferences on the mound. Who in the hell would have a clue what they were saying to one another unless you were a Navajo?"

"Now that you mention it," says Klein, "I remember reading about Navajos who served in the United States Marine Corps and manned the telephones and radios for military telecommunication. They were known as 'code talkers,' who spoke in their native language with coded words that confused the Japanese since they were unable to decipher them."

As for the major league club, the Orioles managed to climb out of the cellar and contend with the dreaded Yankees and Red Sox until the last week of the season, losing four straight games and fading to third place in the final standings. The familiar refrain "Wait until next year" was echoed by their fans.

However, after the season is over, Mr. Dunn tells Chubby to report to him as soon as possible. "Based on the recommendation from Joe Klein," Mr. Dunn tells him, "we're offering you a job as a free-lance scout, a big title with little pay, but if you find another prospect like Bigfoot, your salary will double. You're just a 'bird dog,' son, but it's a start and you'll be around the game that you love."

"Thank you, Mr. Dunn," says Chubby. "When you sign one of my boys, they will take a little bit of me with them on their way to the big leagues. I don't know what to call it, but it's damned satisfying to me and you can't put a price on it."

When Chubby returns to Ridgefield to continue the rehabilitation on his wrist, he occasionally jogs into the Wildlife Refuge. At noon he's forged a friendship with three Red-Breasted Robins, which he calls '*The Bobbin' Robins.*' He's teaching them to sing one of his old favorites, '*Mr. Sandman, Bring Me a Dream,*' except the lyrics are changed to '*bring me a doll.*' Between therapy exercises on his injured wrist, this 25-year old farm boy finds a special peace inside the Refuge and bides his time until he can grip a baseball without pain in his fingers. Pretty girls are always on his mind, even flirting with *The Bobbin' Robins*, who he claims, 'harmonize a *helluva* lot better than the *Oryuls* play baseball.'

Around Thanksgiving Day Chubby receives a letter, postmarked Charlotte, North Carolina, and with a distinct whiff of perfume on the paper. It's from Acela Lori, who apologizes for not writing sooner but was busy trying to find a job and embarrassed to tell anyone outside of her family that she was working at Burger King. She mentions the fun they had during their train ride from Washington DC to Charlotte. In the middle of the letter she says that she has been following the *O's* and looking for an update after learning about his injury that put him on the disabled list. Her letter ends with an invitation to meet her family and catch up on a guessing game that was never finished on the train. She writes as a conclusion: "I'm an old movie buff and close this letter with something Rick Blaine (Humphrey Bogart) said to Captain Louis Renault (Claude Rains) in *Casablanca*: 'This could be the start of a beautiful friendship.'"

CHAPTER 15

It's Thanksgiving Day at Cylburn. Twenty guests from Ridgefield and Sparrows Point are invited for a turkey dinner with all the trimmings. If Norman Rockwell was there, he would have set his easel off to one side of the room and created an illustration for the cover of *Maryland Life* Magazine.

While most of the women are in the kitchen helping Sara, Mark is holding court in the drawing room, explaining his latest acquisition in art to Reggie, York, Sergio and Womble. "Here's a wonderful example, circa 1920, by Gardner Symons, an artist who is associated with the New Hope colony of artists," says Mark with conviction. "There was no information on the back of the painting or frame, so I've titled it "Early Morning Light in the Berkshires."

"Growing up in Bucks County near Main and Bridge Streets near the Playhouse in downtown New Hope," says York, "I don't think a day went by without someone mentioning the importance of those artists. Symons was considered a master of *plein-air* painting."

"Did you have to twist the arm of the seller in order to buy it?" asks Womble with a chuckle.

"No twisting of arms, but more like arm-wrestling or mind-wrestling," says Mark. "I bought it from an estate in New Jersey. It was *touch-and-go* there for a while because the owner, recently widowed, told me it was a wedding present when she and her husband married for the second time about thirty years ago.

"Early Morning Light in the Berkshires, c. 1920" by George Gardner Symons (American 1861-1930)

She was well-endowed, financially speaking, and didn't need the money, but showed great skill in the bargaining process."

"Did you eventually hand her a blank check and ask her to fill in the amount?" asks Reggie.

"She was too refined a lady, so I tried to tell her what her painting meant to me."

"And?" asks Sergio, pronouncing the word the way a baritone would sing it.

"I told her that I could hear music coming from the unpredictable ripples in the stream as water flowed over a bed of stones," says Mark. "It sounded like a jazz riff from the piano keyboard of Stan Kenton. She was puzzled and never heard of him or his band. So I told her the painting also reminded me of poems by Robert Frost."

"Don't tell me she never heard of Frost?" asks York.

"She nodded her head nonchalantly, then I proceeded to quote some words from his epitaph: 'I had a lover's quarrel with the world,' then added my own suffix: 'I also had a love affair with God's bountiful nature.'"

"For God's sake, please spare me the assignations and explain how you convinced her to sell you the Symons painting?" asks York, exasperated. "My hair is beginning to turn gray."

"Reflecting on Robert Frost didn't seem to sway her one way or another," says Mark, enjoying the rapt attention of his group, "and my heart was skipping a beat. So I tried to appeal to her business acumen and explained some of the problems if she were to place her Symons painting on consignment with a gallery or auction house. She was still reluctant to part with it, even after my guaranteeing it would be given a place of honor and respect in my home. Then she surprised me by asking: 'What happens if you decide to sell it later for a very big price?'"

"Is this when you applied some mind-wrestling?" asks Sergio, becoming antsy.

"As I said before," says Mark, "she was well-off financially but holding tightly onto the memory of a wedding gift."

"Did you tell her, you'd divorce your wife and marry her?" asks Sergio with a snicker.

"Gentlemen, that's enough questions for now," says Mark "What happened next or how I pried it away is another story for another time. It could make an interesting episode in our next film at Ridgefield."

"I hope one day I can be as smart as you and make one or two million, whichever comes first!" says Sergio. "I just have to keep at it, no matter how long it takes."

Concurrently, in the kitchen, most of the women are busy helping Sara, who is more of a traffic cop telling who to do what, when and where. In all the commotion, no one is paying any attention to 5-year-old Jamie, who reaches into a bowl of nuts and puts a fistful in his mouth. A minute later he is flinging his hands wildly and choking on one that has clogged his windpipe. Jen, their 8-year old golden lab, notices his contortions and begins to bark so loudly that it draws the attention of Glen Glenn, who happens to be walking past the kitchen door.

Glen rushes over to Jaime, leaning his head over the back of a chair. He bends down behind him and places his right fist, thumb side in, just below his rib cage in the front. He grabs his fist with the other hand and, keeping his arms off Jaime's rib cage, gives four quick inward and upward thrusts. He repeats it twice before the large nut is coughed out.

Glen's quick thinking and action saved Jaime's life. When Mark is told of the incident, he becomes teary. "How can I ever repay you?" he asks Glen, feeling a sense of guilt for not paying more attention to Jaime.

"You gave me a second chance after trying to pick your pocket at Lexington Market," he tells Mark, gratefully. "Thank God, Jen barked when she did."

Mark carries Jamie in his arms and asks Glen to follow them into his study. "I want to be alone with Jaime," he tells Glen. "See that no one disturbs me for a few minutes, please." He reclines in his *Eames* lounge chair, with Jaime sitting on his stomach, and kisses the St. Christopher medal around his neck.

"I gave this medal to Ruth on the day I married her and put it around your little neck on the day I buried her," he tells him. "If you say your prayers every day, it will continue to protect you, just as it has a few moments ago. God has been good to you and to everyone who loves you."

Then Mark begins to sing softly:

> *"Oh Jaime boy, the bells, the bells are ringing, from glen to glen and down the mountain side, the summer's gone and all the roses falling, yes it's you, yes you who's still with me alive. Yes, we're going to see the meadow or soon the valley's hushed with snow, yes, we'll be together again in sunshine or shadow, oh Jaime boy, oh Jaime boy, I love you so."*

Jaime grabs hold of Mark's neck and kisses him.

"Is there anything you want to say?" asks Mark.

"Why didn't someone tell me to take the shell off a pistachio nut before eating it?"

Jen scratches the bottom of the door then pushes it wide enough to fit her 80-pound body through the opening. She takes a few steps, puts her front paws on the lounge chair and begins to lick Jamie's face. He giggles and playfully tries to grab hold of her ears. But Jen keeps moving her head and wagging her tail until Mark intervenes and tells her, "I'll never again tell you to go to your room and stay out of my affairs, Jennie girl."

Fifteen minutes later, after everyone settles down at the dinner table, Mark rises to make a special Thanksgiving toast. "Jaime might not be alive if I hadn't brought Jen to Cylburn and hadn't met Glen Glenn at Lexington Market," he tells them, raising his glass of champagne high above his head. "Philosopher Yogi Berra says, 'It's never over 'til it's over,' and for friends like *ya'll* here today, there will never be enough hours in the day to express our appreciation for all you've done for us. My seven years at Betterton and Rock Hall are a distant memory but they will never be forgotten."

Following dinner, Reggie invites everyone to the library where the women are offered seats while the men stand behind them and loosen their belts. Before taking his seat at the baby grand, Richard hands Reggie his guitar. "From the Hippodrome stage to Cylburn is a short hop, skip and jump for the *Bettertones*," says Reggie, "but one is headed west next week to begin work on a new weekly television series. He'll play the part of an orderly, a Damon Runyon character with special musical talents. He's our very own Little Mac Brown."

When the applause dies down, Richard tells them, "We were kept in the dark and never knew he auditioned and is on his way to stardom. His seven years with us at Ridgefield are ancient history. Next week he'll be singing melodies in a style reminiscent of Sam Cooke, with arrangements written especially for him by Reggie and me."

Reggie motions Little Mac, Sandy and Liz to come forward, and for the next fifteen minutes, sing and swing to a medley arranged as *soul music*, starting with an arrangement of *Wonderful World*. The music is the same as written for Sam Cooke in 1960, but now given a new title, *What a Fabulous World It Would Be* with the following lyrics:

"I know all about antiquity, I know all about topography,
I know all about sociality, and the same for psychology,
I'll never forget accounting 1-0-1, and the gains and losses, honey bon,
but I don't know if you love me, nothing ever suits you or me to a T,
if things were perfect, what a fabulous world it would be."

While Reggie and the *Bettertones* are performing, Sergio Leone Jr., signals his cameraman James Wong Howe Jr. to begin shooting Little Mac's performance for use in a possible film project at Ridgefield.

After the session ends, everyone gathers in a semi-circle around Little Mac to hear about his new *gig*. "Tell us more about where you're going and what you'll be doing after you get there," says York.

"For starters, I'll be working at a high-class health spa built in the Badlands of Montana near Little Big Horn. The resort, owned by a consortium of Cheyenne, Lakota, Arapaho and Sioux tribes, is called Bad Custerville."

"That name has a familiar ring to it," says Womble.

"It's patterned after the classy Baden-Baden, a playground for the very rich in the Black Forest of Germany," says Little Mac. "It's designed for those who want to experience the thrill of a casino and take the *Kur* – a bath in the hot mineral springs, sauna, massage and long walks to ease the tension in your mind."

"You sound like a barker from the Old West, promoting a newfangled liniment with healing powers," says Annette.

"We're forgetting that Little Mac was a reporter for *The Sun* who worked as a paralegal for Mike and me while getting his degree from UB Law School," says Lola.

"Four hours a day, Monday through Thursday, I'll be working as an orderly, helping rich people lose excess fat around their waist."

"And on the weekends?" asks Sandy.

"Friday and Saturday nights I'll be joining two girls from the chorus line. We're the *Bobbin' Robbins* and we'll give a live variety show for HBO, with Gene Wilder as MC Emeritus. If you think he was funny in *Blazing Saddles*, wait until you see him as the sheriff-psychologist of *Custer's Saloon*," says Little Mac.

"It couldn't happen to a better guy," says Abigail. "I mean you, not Gene Wilder. When you cut your first record, send me a copy and I'll assume the role of *song peddler* and try to get it played on the radio stations around here."

"Seems as if the Indians are getting some revenge for what the American government and U.S. cavalry did to them over a hundred years ago," says Liz."

"American Indians were always clever business people," says Little Mac, "but made mistakes trusting the white man. With their new casinos, they will have slots and game tables set up to relieve wealthy compulsive gamblers of excess cash from their wallets."

"How about arranging for Eloise and me to open a trading post?" asks Womble.

"You're a few years too late," says Little Mac. "You should see their trading post. It's *Tiffany's of the West*, with the best of Indian blankets, jewelry, pottery and artifacts."

As soon as Little Mac ends his *spiel*, Reggie tells everyone that Lois Carnegie would like to have the last word and motions her to come forward.

"It is not my intention to steal the spotlight from all the exciting things happening today," says Lois, "but Mark and I felt that Thanksgiving would be the right moment to tell you about a donation in memory of one of our co-workers. First, Mark and his family have established a trust for the education of the children of Captain Jones, who lost his life at the mill. Secondly, I have donated to the Baltimore Museum of Art a beautiful painting of Arabian horses that has been handed down in the Carnegie family from the time it was purchased directly from the artist in 1869. It's a masterpiece by the German artist Adolf Schreyer, titled *The Attack*. It will be exhibited in their gallery of nineteenth century European art and bear the label, 'Donated by the staff of Bethlehem Steel in loving memory of Captain Jones.' Mark and I felt the need to perpetuate the name of a brave man who gave his life trying to save the mill from further disaster."

The Attack, painted by Adolf Schreyer (German 1828-1899).

Chapter 16

While everyone is charged with excitement inside the R&D Lab at Ridgefield, C. Alvin Kissinger, the 40-year old bachelor whose life is dedicated to JTTF and devoted to his boss Buster Browne, is rolling back and forth in his bed inside his cozy but small condo overlooking the Inner Harbor. He eventually wakes up from another nightmare about Rook's last hours alive. He can't reconcile some comments made *off-the-cuff* by the butler in a subsequent interview in the library of Rook's mansion. The comments stream across his mind in the middle of the night. Being a persistent cuss, he feels the nightmares might be resolved by having a closer look at the file in his computer. He puts on a robe, drags his feet in sloppy bedroom slippers to his study and falls into a chair. After logging in, he opens the file on Rook and stops scrolling a minute later when a photo taken with a Panoscan camera clearly shows him stretched out on the platform of his model train display; Rook is dressed in the uniform of a train conductor, with one hand gripping a conductor's cap and the other inside a bag of tortilla chips. "Something doesn't make sense," he says to himself. "The butler told me that he never ate avocadoes, so how in the hell did he get hold of a bag of chips?"

Around 8:00 a.m., C. Alvin marches into Buster's office to get his permission to talk to the DA. "It's a personal matter," he tells him. "I'll explain it all later if you don't mind. All I can tell you at this point is, almost a year after Rook's death, lawyers are still trying to entangle viability and liability issues of Rook and his conspirators who took part in the sabotage of Bethlehem Steel. Millions of dollars are at stake from Rook's estate, and the attorneys for Bethlehem Steel want the mill to be compensated before the state takes a bite *outta* it."

A few hours later, after conferring with the DA, C. Alvin is upbeat and behind the wheel of his car on the road to interview the two union thugs at the Federal Correctional Institution (FCI), a minimum-security prison in Cumberland, Maryland.

The following morning at 7:00 a.m., when Buster passes C. Alvin's office, he finds his top aide wearing his favorite battered blue-serge jacket and tapping the keyboard of his computer. "What's up, Doc?" Buster asks.

"You're not going to believe what I discovered."

"If you know something and want me to know it, then spit it out before I split open your head with a karate blow."

"Funny you should say that, because that's the exact words they used when they went to Rook to collect the money for sabotaging the mill."

"Who went where to collect what?" asks Buster, growing impatient.

"The two union thugs. A week after lying low, they went to Rook to collect the money he owed them for sabotaging of the mill."

"I wish you'd stop using that old cliché. These are important characters and you should reveal their names."

"The tall, slim one is Vladimir 'Push' Pushkin. The short, squatty one is Leon 'Shuv' Shuvnikov. Both are musclemen – enforcers -- who were part of a smaller core of over-active, ambitious union members."

"Paid professionals?"

"Absolutely, and hard-headed to boot," says C. Alvin. "They considered themselves *Bolsheviks* and told me there wasn't a day when they didn't work and weren't hungry."

"O.K. I get the picture. What does this have to do with Rook?"

"According to them, Rook was in a playful mood and dressed as a conductor of the B&O Railroad when they went to his mansion to collect their money for sabotaging the steel mill. To their shock and horror he was reluctant to pay them off and denied any involvement in the sabotage. They reasoned and pleaded with him, explaining that everything was recorded on their cell."

"Now you're getting somewhere," says Buster.

"When he stalled, they told him they meant business and offered him the choice of handing over the cash or facing a split down the center of his head. Rook laughed when they called it a 50-50 split, meaning fifty grand for each of them. Then they told me Rook took the bag of chips from one of them and asked them to have a seat while he went for the money."

"Are you shitting me?"

"After waiting about ten minutes, they said they couldn't get into his study because Rook had locked the door. They left the mansion after Rook assured them he would have all the cash tomorrow night."

Buster finds a chair and collapses in it.

"Before they confessed everything to me," says C. Alvin, "I had to get an affidavit from the DA, signed by the judge, to give them immunity from further prosecution for the murder of Les Rook. It was not something they planned to do. They said those last days inside Rook's mansion were constantly on their mind. They were dying to tell someone, anyone that they had nothing to do with Rook's death. As I was leaving the interrogation room, they also asked me if they can sue his estate for 'accounts payable' since Rook never paid them. They said that they could use the $100,000 after they serve their time in prison."

"Incredible."

"At least now we can put an exclamation point to the story behind the story of Rook's death," says C. Alvin, reaching into a bag of tortilla chips on his desk, taking one and passing the bag to Buster. "Ever tried them, Chief? These are sprinkled with hot chili peppers and are guaranteed to put some pep in your step."

"That was decent of them to come clean when they could have clammed up like an oyster. What made them conceal all this material from the DA and reveal it openly to you?" asks Buster, scratching his head.

"After we were seated, I looked directly into their eyes, told them of evidence that could send them to the electric chair and asked why they were shielding someone since they weren't smart enough to concoct the sabotage. Eventually I asked them who they were protecting and if they were ready to come clean."

"Go on."

"I leaned forward and asked them to bow their heads while I said a prayer over them in Latin."

"And?"

"I asked them straight out: 'Tell me, my sons, how and why you did it?'"

"You *sonofa* bitch," says Buster, losing his patience. "If you keep me in suspense any longer, I'll kick you from here to M&T Stadium."

"They said, 'it wasn't easy,'" says C. Alvin. "Oh, didn't I tell you? How foolish of me to forget to explain it all. To gain their complete confidence I wore a high-white collar above a dark suit and posed as a clergy man. They even thanked me for giving them absolution after they came clean!"

"You what?"

"I saw nothing wrong with it since everything they said to me was off the record and could never be used in court," says C. Alvin, bowing his head, folding his hands in prayer and making the sign of the cross. "And I don't believe God would object to my being a disciple to get at the truth."

"A discombobulating development," says Buster, tilting his head downward to look over his spectacles at C. Alvin. "Very perceptive of you."

"Tenacious and persistent, just like the devil," says C. Alvin. "Do you believe that everything in life is preordained?"

"Never gave it much thought since so much of our work is based on science," says Buster with exasperation in his voice. "Now you're getting into philosophy, which for me is like trying to walk through quicksand."

"A confession is soothing to the soul," says C. Alvin, glowing proudly that his nightmares should disappear. "But I should be able to get a good night's sleep without thinking any more about how Rook died."

"You *sonofa* bitch," says Buster, puzzled and not knowing whether to howl or burst out laughing. He falls into a chair in front of C. Alvin's desk and tells him, "I made you my top aide because you could always resolve the unresolvable. You started as a soldier down in the trenches, working undercover with no fear of the fight or consequences. I think you're ready to take over as chief of the bureau. It's time for me to retire before I have a heart attack."

"You should cut down on your cups of coffee a day," says C. Alvin. "Too much caffeine gives you more mood swings than Duke Ellington's *Mood Indigo.*

"I'll take it under advisement," says Buster.

"One more bit of advice, Chief," says C. Alvin. "Never give a sucker or two suckers like *Push* and *Shuv* an even break!"

Chapter 17

On the first Saturday of May, after enjoying a lunch of soft shell crabs, sautéed in butter and chardonnay, Abigail is relaxing inside her study on Charles Street, with her feet propped up on an ottoman. After closing her eyes for a minute or two, she reaches for her cell and speed dials Mark. "I expected the labor of writing a non-fiction book about Rex Ingram would be similar to my master's thesis," she says, "but it's tormenting because of the challenge to adhere to the truth and keep my opinions to myself. For every answer to a previous question, two different questions pop up. In other words, for every step forward to uncover new info, I'm taking two steps backward because of questions only a dead man can answer."

"You have an adventurous imagination," says Mark. "Your frustration and struggle is no different than what writers like Steinbeck and Hemingway experienced when writing their books."

"It's almost impossible to suppress my conscience and opinions," says Abigail. "At the end of the week, after I make revision after revision, very little is saved in my file. So far, all I can show for a month's labor is the fat forming around my waist from sitting at my computer. Would you mind if I could drop by within the next hour to discuss another project that may be a better use of my time and energy?"

After Mark invites her to come right over, it takes less than 15 minutes for her to drive to Cylburn since her condo is only four miles away. "What a beautiful painting you have hanging on that far wall," says Abigail, being ushered into his study. "I never noticed it before."

"Corner of My Garden" by William Henry Singer, Jr.
(American 1868-1943)

"That's because we recently removed it from storage and had it cleaned of old varnish," says Mark. "Do you recognize the artist?"

"I thought the brushstroke was familiar," says Abigail. "We have a number of his paintings donated to WCMFA in Hagerstown, his wife's birthplace in the Cumberland region."

"It's one of my mother's favorites."

"It's a fabulous work by William Henry Singer, Jr.," says Abigail. "He was born in Pittsburg in 1868. His father was a co-founder of the Singer-Nimick Steel Works and later became a partner of

Andrew Carnegie in the 1890's. In fact, Carnegie was one of the first collectors to buy a Singer painting after they met accidentally during a transatlantic ship crossing."

"It's always puzzling to me," says Mark, "as to why someone growing up in Pittsburgh and graduating with a degree in accounting from Carnegie Institute would suddenly leave his destiny as owner of a steel mill and pursue an interest as a landscape painter."

"I can offer several reasons but would prefer to know more about how you acquired it."

"This painting has been in the family since 1916," says Mark, "when my grandfather bought it after being exhibited at the Carnegie Exhibition in Pittsburgh. It's a masterpiece, titled *Corner of My Garden*, which reminded him of his garden here at Cylburn. But you didn't come here to discuss our Singer painting. What's on your mind?"

"I've been laboring over my book about Rex Ingram and realized that I may have to put it on hold."

"Why is that?" asks Mark, growing more inquisitive.

"Blame it on Dixon's, damn it. Pardon my language but I just broke a fingernail," says Abigail. "That's what frustration will do to your psyche and fingernails."

"What's going on at Crumpton?" asks Mark, slightly puzzled and curious.

"They're preparing for an auction in two weeks, with over 700 paintings and 400 frames to be sold in one fast-selling session. The sale starts at 2:30 in the afternoon."

"You'll be there until eight at night," Mark says. "Have you previewed it?"

"Yes, regrettably," she answers. "It's the worst pile of junk I've ever seen at auction and I can't figure out why anyone would ever buy it."

"It had to be someone addicted to buying at auction, someone who refused to go home empty handed, like me."

"You mean, like me," she says. "But there's nothing that I would buy and hang on the walls of my condo. Everything is badly in need of restoration."

"I can tell by your cunning smile that you have something in mind about this junk," says Mark.

"What would you say to our launching a conservation studio at Ridgefield, under the direction of an experienced conservator?"

"You might find someone ready to retire from a museum or business and anxious to slow down from the grind of 8:00 AM to 5:00 PM," says Mark.

"The goal would be to hire someone to teach a group of trainees the basic fundamentals of how to clean a painting of grime and old varnish, line it with new linen in a vacuum press when there's a tear or crazing due to poorly formulated varnish, etc. For the first class I envision about 20 interns who could practice on about 200 of those paintings at Crumpton, which can be bought for under $25 each, representing an initial outlay of $5,000. We'd be giving them an education and a job that will pay them above minimum wage, with the prospect of a salaried job later. It might fit into your 'Heads Up' and 'Restart' programs for unemployed workers."

"If it pans out, you could franchise it all over America," says Mark. "Think of how many jobs could be created and how much art could be rescued from the trash heap of floods, tornadoes, hurricanes and earthquakes."

"So you feel the project has some merit?" asks Abigail.

"It's worth pursuing if you can hire the right person to manage the lab and the best conservator to teach the beginners," says Mark. "Remember, some of those chemicals are toxic and require proper care and handling, and ventilation. Also you'll need insurance to cover accidents. Discuss it with Womble, although he may not have the time to get involved."

"If you're referring to his involvement with Eloise," says Abigail, "I've watched them form a good bond in business with intellectual properties. It's wonderful to see them prospering on a personal level, too. He's grown very fond of her peaches."

"It goes way beyond his fondness for her peaches," says Mark, laughing. "However, even if you can't get him involved, you have my complete financial backing to proceed."

"I have another thought that just crossed my mind. Once the word gets out -- and sooner or later it will -- someone might bring us a painting to restore, possibly one worth over $5,000. It would be something like a Treasure Day Open House that auction houses schedule in cities all over America. Being an optimist, I suspect we could offer them half of what's it worth, restore it and list it on our gallery over the Internet."

"Not only list it but open a gallery at Ridgefield. When someone responds and wants to see it, they pay the cost of their travel to BWI, where you meet and drive them to one of the trailers behind the main house. You can include lunch and dinner with Gaby's fluffy crepes and Capt'n Chucky's distinctive back-fin crab cake platters from Newton Square, Pennsylvania. If they buy the painting at full price, all their expenses will be deducted from the sale."

"If we're their host, why not give them a tour of the Wildlife Refuge next door, too? In a way we'd be promoting the Eastern Shore of Maryland," says Abigail, taking a deep breath. "I'm not surprised by the way you can grab an idea and plunge forward with it, like a handoff from Joe Flacco to Ray Rice."

"I wasn't aware that you were a *Ravens* fan."

"I find it relaxing to give the sports pages of *The Sun* a cursory look," she says. "Now, if the *Orioles* could find a way to beat the *Yankees* and *Red Sox,* that'd be something to smile about."

"It's only the first month of the baseball season and you're asking for a miracle. But speaking of 'getting serious' and 'prospering,' have you heard about *Stormy Alex* running in the Preakness Stakes at Pimlico?" asks Mark.

"That is good news," says Abigail. "I knew about your ownership with Tom Bowman, but wasn't aware that *Stormy Alex* is now a three-year-old and the third Saturday in May is just around the corner."

"*Stormy Alex* has been training under Dr. Tom Bowman, who said he's anxious to show the world what he can do on the racetrack. I mean *Stormy Alex* is anxious, not Doc Bowman."

"I read Doc was teary-eyed when *Stormy Alex* had to be withdrawn from the Kentucky Derby because of a lung infection."

"He was also wary-eyed from being his vet 24 hours a day for three years," says Mark. "Doc kept me advised and it was hit-and-miss for a few days, not knowing how *Stormy Alex* would respond to medications. Frankly, I don't know anyone at 77 who could have faced the dangerous decisions and never flinched; it was incredibly onerous. Doc is short and crusty on the outside, but virile and sweet on the inside. I couldn't ask for a better partner."

"If I was Greta looking into a crystal ball, I'd say that it won't surprise me if *Stormy Alex* wins by a nose in a photo finish."

"You believe it will be that close a race?"

"No. I believe that *Stormy Alex* likes to beat the competition, not show them up. From what I've read in *The Sun*, he waits for his jockey to tap him then bursts with all his power and might to weave through the pack to take the lead, a lead he rarely relinquishes."

The following weekend Mark has his arm around Tom Bowman's shoulder. "Here we are leaning on the railing of Dance Forth Farms and watching our *big hossy take* his final tune-up before going to Pimlico."

"He looks so much stronger and eager to show off a little," says Bowman. "This is the day I've been dreaming about all my life."

"I can't believe it's been three years from the night you offered me a share in the ownership of *Stormy Alex*," says Mark, pulling the much shorter trainer closer to him. "I still get that *high* like I did as a SEAL heading into unchartered waters."

"I've got the same feeling, son," says Bowman. "This race at Pimlico represents my love affair with horse-racing and a bold gamble to keep breeders in Maryland from being lured to neighboring states such as Pennsylvania and Delaware, where purses are much bigger for Thoroughbreds born there."

"I wish people would stop talking about tradition," says Mark. "Hell, tradition is passé when it comes to investing big bucks in the Sport of Kings."

"People forget the long hours I've spent as a vet and trainer caring for *Stormy Alex*," says Tom. "Sixteen hands, 1,100 pounds around lungs the size of watermelons, is a lot to care for, but I'm not complaining. When you see *big hossy* toss his head back to look into your eyes, he seems to be saying, 'It will all be worth it someday, Doc.'"

"In ten days, says Mark, "we'll be racing on the same one-mile-and-three-sixteenths track as *Man o' War, Seabiscuit, War Admiral, Citation, Secretariat and Cigar*."

"You mean *Stormy Alex* will be racing, not you," says Doc, laughing for the first time in days. "I can see our gray colt covered with a blanket of Black-Eyed Susan's in the Winner's Circle."

"Anything special you'll tell *Stormy Alex* in the paddock before the race starts?" asks Mark, curiously.

"Never gave it a thought. The owners and trainers talk with the jockey, not the horse," says Doc, grinning. "But since you asked, I'd tell him, 'When the going gets tough, the tough get going,' then wait for his trademark neigh, meaning 'let's get this show on the road, Doc.' And you?"

"I'll pat his firm withers, kiss him under his eye and whisper in his ear, 'This is your day, the chance of a lifetime. Don't hold back. Fly as if the wind coming up the Chesapeake Bay is lifting you off the ground.'"

THE END

GLOSSARY GUIDE

(Compiled by the author and inspired by Gordon Beard who published his "Basic Baltimorese" in 1979, '90 and '99.)

Pronunciation (Slang)	**Correct Spelling**
Aba-deen	Aberdeen
amblanz	ambulance
Anne-Arunnel	Anne Arundel
anytink	anything
apt-tight	appetite
arn	iron
arster	oyster
arthur	author
Ay-rabb	Arab
baffroom	bathroom
Bawlamer, Bawlmer	Baltimore
beero	bureau
betcha	bet you
Bethum Steel	Bethlehem Steel
Betterin	Betterton

bin	been
Blair	Belair
bob-war	bobbed-wire
bootiful	beautiful
boybin	bourbon
bray-edd	bread
burn	born
Cha-lee	Charlie
Chesspeake	Chesapeake
Clumya	Columbia
complected	complexioned
cornner	coroner
corter	quarter
Curt's Bay	Curtis Bay
curup	corrupt
curyus	curious
curyusty	curiosity
dare	there
dee-smissed	dismissed
doll	dial
Droodle Hill	Druid-Hill
dubya	w
Dundock	Dundalk
ee-light	elite
eht	eat
es-choo-air-ree	estuary
excape	escape
faloo	flu
far	fire
Fert Mckenny	Fort McHenry

fillum	film
fur	for
Furd	Ford
furty	forty
gaden	garden
gabage	garbage
Glenin	Glyndon
goff	golf
goldie	goalie
Greenmont	Greenmount
guvner	governor
hafta	have to
har	hire
harber	harbor
harble	horrible
harred	hired
Harrid	Howard
Harrid Street	Howard Street
helluva	hell of a
Hippdrum	Hippodrome
hosbiddle	hospital
hoss	horse
i-deer	idea
igger	eager
iggle	eagle
ig-nert	ignorant
incabate	incubate
Inna Harber	Inner Harbor
inner-rested	interested
inner-restin	interesting

jiggered	jagged
jografee	geography
jools	jewels
keerful	careful
kidney gaden	kindergarten
kroddy	karate
Liddle Itly	Little Italy
lie-berry	library
lig	league
Luck's Point	Locust Point
Lumbered Street	Lombard Street
mavalus	marvelous
mare	mayor
member	remember
mezz-aline	mezzanine
moran pie	meringue pie
Murlin	Maryland
Naplis	Annapolis
neck store	next door
noh	no
notink	nothing
od-a-sey *orning*	odyssey awning
Oryuls	Orioles
pa-lease	please
Patapsico	Patapsco
Patomac	Patomac
pawtrit	portrait
postcad	postcard
payment	pavement

Plaski	Pulaski
plooshin	pollution
po-leece	police
quairyum	aquarium
quarr	choir
Recerstown	Reisterstown
roolty	royalty
rower skates	roller-skates
rown	around
Sagmor	Sagamore
sec-er-terry	secretary
Sigh-a-neye	Sinai
sil-lo-kwee	soliloquy
smat	smart
sometink	something
sore	sewer
sore asses	psoriasis
Sparris Point	Sparrows Point
spicket	spigot
Talzin	Towson
tarpoleon	tarpaulin
tink	thing
tuhmar	tomorrow
Tulla	Tallulah
twunny	twenty
uhpair	up there
umpar	umpire
urshter	oyster
Vandabill	Vanderbilt
varse	worse

vollince	violence
vydock	viaduct
warder	water
Warshtin	Washington
Westminster	Westminster
Whataya	What do you
whirl	world
winder	window
wit	with
wrench	rinse
Wuff Street	Wolfe Street
x-lint	excellent
x-raided	x-rated
ya	you
yella	yellow
yesterday	yesterday
yewmid	humid
yewmity	humidity
yur	you're, you are
Yurp	Europe
yursell	yourself
zackly	exactly
zinc	sink

Correct Spelling	***Pronunciation (Slang)***
Aberdeen	*Aba-deen*
ambulance	*amblanz*
Annapolis	*Naplis*
Anne Arundel	*Anne Arunnel*
anything	*anytink*
appetite	*apt-tight*
aquarium	*quairyum*
Arab	*Ay-rabb*
around	*rown*
author	*arthur*
awning	*orning*
Baltimore	*Bawlamer, Bawlmer*
bathroom	*baffroom*
beautiful	*bootiful*
been	*bin*
bet you	*betcha*
Betterton	*Betterin*
blue	*ba-lu*
bobbed wire	*bobwar*
born	*burn*
bourbon	*boybin*
bread	*bray-edd*
buoy	*boe-way*
bureau	*beero*
Belair	*Blair*
Bethlehem Steel	*Bethum Steel*
careful	*keerful*
Charlie	*Cha-lee*

Chesapeake	*Chesspeake*
choir	*quarr*
Columbia	*Clumya*
complexioned	*complected*
coroner	*cornner*
corrupt	*curup*
curious	*curyus*
curiosity	*curyusty*
Curtis Bay	*Curt's Bay*
dial	*doll*
dismissed	*de-smissed*
Druid Hill	*Droodle Hill*
Dundalk	*Dundock*
eager	*igger*
eagle	*iggle*
eat	*eht*
elite	*ee-light*
escape	*excape*
estuary	*es-choo-air-ree*
Europe	*Yurp*
exactly	*zackly*
explain	*splain*
February	*Febrarie*
film	*fillum*
fire	*far*
fireaway	*farway*
flu	*faloo*
Ford	*Furd*
for	*fur*
Fort McHenry	*Fert Mekenny*

forty	*furty*
garbage	*gabage*
garden	*Gaden*
geography	*jografee*
golf	*goff*
Glyndon	*Glenin*
goalie	*goldie*
Gough Street	*Guff Street*
governor	*guvner*
Greenmount	*Greenmont*
harbor	*harber*
have to	*hafta*
heard	*hoyd*
hell of a	*helluva*
Hippodrome	*Hippdrum*
hire	*har*
hired	*harred*
horse	*hoss*
horrible	*harble*
hospital	*hosbiddle*
Howard	*Harrid*
incubate	*incabate*
Inner Harbor	*Inna Harber*
interested	*inner-rested*
interesting	*inner-restin*
iron	*arn*
jagged	*jaggered*
jewels	*jools*
karate	*kroddy*
kindergarten	*kidneygaden*

league	*lig*
library	*lie-berry*
Little Italy	*Liddle Eitly*
Locust Point	*Luck's Pernt*
Lombard Street	*Lumbered Street*
marvelous	*mavalus*
Maryland	*Murlin*
mayor	*mare*
meringue pie	*moran pie*
mezzanine	*mezz-aline*
next door	*neck store*
no	*nope*
nothing	*notink*
odyssey Orioles	*od-a-sey* *Oryuls*
oyster	*arster, urshter*
Patapsco	*Patapsico*
Patomac	*Potomac*
pavement	*payment*
please	*pa-lease*
police	*po-leece*
pollution	*plooshin*
portrait	*pawtrit*
postcard	*postcad*
psoriasis	*sore asses*
Pulaski	*Plaski*
quarter	*corter*
Reisterstown	*Ricerstown*
remember	*member*
rinse	*rench, wrench*

roller-skates	*rower-skates*
royalty	*roolty*
Sagamore	*Sagmor*
secretary	*sec-er-terry*
sewer	*sore*
Sinai	*Sigh-a-neye*
sink	*zinc*
smart	*smat*
soliloquy	*sil-lo-kwee*
something	*sometink*
spigot	*spicket*
Sparrows Point	*Sparris Point*
Tallulah	*Tulla*
tarpaulin	*tarpoleon*
there	*dare*
thing	*tink*
tomorrow	*tuhmar*
Towson	*Talzin*
twenty	*twunny*
umpire	*umpar*
up there	*uhpair*
Vanderbilt	*Vandabill*
viaduct	*vydock*
violence	*vollince*
w	*dubya*
war	*wah*
Washington	*Warshtin*
water	*warder*
Westminster	*Wesminister*
what do you	*whataya*

window	*winder*
with	*wit*
Wolfe Street	*Wuff Street*
world	*whirl*
worse	*varse*
excellent	*x-lint*
x-rated	*x-raided*
yellow	*yella*
yesterday	*yeserdy*
you	*ya*
you are	*yur*
yourself	*Yourself*

An Afterthought

(For the readers of ***BETTERTON***, ***ROCK HALL***, ***ABERDEEN*** and ***SPARROWS POINT***)

"Pay attention for you is now one of my flock of sheep,
On your way home, check your GPS for a loud beep,
Always install a new battery pack to keep its performance at a peak,
So that during your lifetime you will find everything you seek."
(Any mistakes in grammar are due to Microsoft Word 2010.)

ART INDEX

All works of art illustrated in *SPARROWS POINT* are currently in the collection of the author, with the following details:

Figure 1 "Napoleon III on a Fox Hunt, 1865-66," painted by Gustave Parquet (Born 1826 in Beauvais, France), oil on canvas, 32 x 25 ¾ inches, signed lower left and annotated "Compiegne Fontainebleau 1865-1866"

Figure 2 Joseph William Szymanski (American 1906-2002). Father of the author.

Figure 3 "The Broncho Buster," a bronze by Frederic Remington (American 1861-1909), 23 ½ inches high, cast by Roman Bronze Works, New York.

Figure 4 "Java Temple Dancer, c.1958," painted by Antonio Blanco (Born 1927 in Manila, Philippines), oil on canvas, 35 x 24 inches, signed lower left.

Figure 5 "Preliminary Trial of a Horse Thief –Scene in a *Western Justice's Court*, c. 1876," painted by John Mulvany (American 1844-1906), 48 x 72 inches, signed lower right.

Figure 6 "The Attack," painted by Adolf Schreyer (German 1828-1899), 34 x 47 inches, signed lower right.

Figure 7 "Early Morning Light in the Berkshires, c. 1920" painted by George Gardner Symons (American 1861-1930), 25 x 30 inches, signed lower left.

Figure 8 "Corner of My Garden, c. 1912" painted by William Henry Singer, Jr. (American 1868-1943), oil on canvas, 39 x 41 ¾ inches, signed lower right.

Inquiries about prints available for sale may be directed to the author at cme4arts@gmail.com.